SOMETHING MOVED

Kit strained at the far edge of the hollow, seeing only by starlight now, waiting, hardly breathing. The form of a man appeared on the lighter-colored dirt of the hollow. Then another crawled up beside him. One by one Cheyenne appeared as if out of nowhere. They gathered around the rim, remaining for a while as motionless as the rocks of the moon. Then one of them moved, not down into the hollow as Kit suspected he might, but along its hard ridge, making his way slowly.

Kit and the others would have only a few seconds once the stalking Cheyenne sounded the alarm. Kit quietly put the rifle to his shoulder and steadied its sights on the crouching man, but he dared not cock it yet. In this absolute silence, drawing back the heavy hammer would be like ringing an alarm bell.

The Indian hovered there a moment, crouched like a cat about to pounce, then a knife appeared in his hand and he leaped....

KIT CARSON

THE COLONEL'S DAUGHTER
DOUG HAWKINS

LEISURE BOOKS ▐▌ NEW YORK CITY

For Douglas Hirt; wonderful writer, great friend, savvy hunting companion.

A LEISURE BOOK®

August 1997

Published by

Dorchester Publishing Co., Inc.
276 Fifth Avenue
New York, NY 10001

Printed in the United States of America.

My sincerest thanks to the late Dr. Thomas Edward, who so graciously allowed me to roam freely through his rare and valuable collection of monographs by that nineteenth-century Native American scholar, Professor W.G.F. Smith.

THE COLONEL'S DAUGHTER

Prologue

"Wiggins was a fraud!" Professor Thomas Edward roared, his long, gnarled finger stabbing out at me from behind the cluttered desk, as if I personally had been responsible for the man's treachery. "And so were all the others: Ike Chamberlain, Solomon Silver, Bob Dempsey . . ." and on went the litany of colorful characters who had romped among the pages of the history books I had just finished reading. I had not quite recovered from his outburst when again he railed, "There never was a band of trappers called 'The Carson Men.' It's all a huge fiction!" he concluded with a long, ragged breath. This was obviously a subject close to his heart.

"But Edwin Sabin—" I started to say, only to be chopped off at the knees.

"Sabin was hoodwinked by that slick talking Oliver Wiggins! But because he had been careful in other areas, reasonably competent researchers who should have known better blithely accepted the Wiggins account." Here the good professor grabbed a fistful of books from

9

the bulging bookcase behind him and slammed them down upon the already overflowing desk. "Estergreen . . . Blackwelder . . . Lavender . . . Vestal . . ."

"Sabin's book sounded quite genuine," I allowed as a sort of peace offering. I had sought out Professor Thomas Edward because of a little article he had written more than twenty years earlier. Being something of a Carson aficionado, I'd discovered the piece while researching a book on Old Bill Williams. Now, with that project out of the way, I'd turned to trace down the sources that Edward had used in his Kit Carson piece.

Past narrowed, shaggy gray eyebrows, the professor stared at me, leaning back into a chair that sent a grating squeak through the small office where the walls all but vanished behind stacks of old papers and cardboard boxes of musty books and journals.

"Sabin was a fiction writer, Mr. Hawkins, just like you." He made it sound as if such creatures were practically beneath contempt. "He should have stuck to his fiction and left history to historians! Now look at the mess he has made for researchers like myself to clean up." The professor seemed to drift into a deep, contemplative state while I glanced around for some means of extricating myself from beneath his unwavering stare.

I cleared my throat. "It appears I have come at a bad time, sir. I think I'll just—"

His tone softened. "No, no, no, please, sit down, Mr. Hawkins." He straightened up in the chair. "I'm afraid we all have our hot buttons. I apologize for mine. Now, why is it you wished to see me?"

I lowered myself onto the well-worn seat of an ancient, leather stool that he had indicated. "It was your piece on Kit Carson. I ran across it while researching another book. It was quite good."

"Thank you, Mr. Hawkins. Coming from a man who earns his living writing popular fiction, I consider that a compliment."

The Colonel's Daughter

"I was curious as to where you had found some of the events you described. I've read the Peters biography, and a few of those other men you just mentioned, but nowhere have I found any mention of the battle upon the Laramie Plains as you described, or the incident with the Sioux in the Black Hills, or that Carson had actually explored Mesa Verde long before Wetherill!"

A small, satisfied smile came to his gaunt face. "We *competent* researchers have our sources," he chirped smugly.

"If you do, then you must have the only copy."

A sudden wariness chilled his gray eyes. "Just what is your point, Mr. Hawkins?"

I didn't let the brusque iciness put me off. "My point is only this. Like those other men you just berated, I do not wish to advance error. I am writing some books about Kit Carson, and I wish to show the true character of the man. Your piece got my natural curiosity revved up, to use a slightly modern phrase." Now it was my turn to lay on the earnestness. "If there are other source materials available, I'd like to know about them."

He stared at me a moment, then abruptly rose to his feet. Edward was a tall man, well over six-three. "I'm sorry I cannot help you, Mr. Hawkins. Now, I have much work to see to."

Reluctantly, I stood up. It wasn't that he *couldn't* help me. The old goat *wouldn't* help me. He had his own private stash of documents hidden away somewhere, and by God, they were going to remain private! Well, I'd run this lead down as far as it was going to go. I could not make him talk if he had it in his thick, *competent* head he wasn't going to. "Thank you for your time, sir," I said, disappointed.

He only stared at me harder as I started for the door.

"Smith." He flung this single name out at me as my hand was upon the doorknob.

"Sir?" I looked back, stuck by the odd glimmer in his eyes, and what seemed to be an internal struggle going on somewhere behind them. With a small twitch of his mouth, he motioned me back to the chair.

"Professor W. G. F. Smith. Ever hear of him?"

I had to admit that I had not.

"Well, I'm not surprised. It was the prejudice of the day, you understand," he added cryptically.

I did not. Then he said something for which I was quite unprepared. "How old would you say I am?"

I'd figured around eighty, but not wanting to insult the man, I guessed low. "Seventy, seventy-five?"

He grinned. "A diplomat, I see. Perhaps politics is your calling, Mr. Hawkins. I shall be ninety-three come May twenty-ninth."

"You don't show it."

"Ah, but I feel it." He eased his lanky frame back into the squeaky chair. "Professor Smith's documents are wonderful first-person accounts of much of Kit Carson's early career. Unfortunately, the few colleagues who have read them have shrugged them off as inconsequential. I, however, have determined their genuineness, and have spent the last fifty years, since acquiring the papers, studying and annotating them. I had hoped someday to produce a new account of Kit Carson based largely upon Professor Smith's manuscripts." He fell into a long silence, and when he spoke again it was with a heavy voice. "Funny how swiftly time slips by." Another long break, then a sudden breath. "Well, none of us lives forever. I have six months."

"I am sorry to hear that, sir." I was curious, of course, but did not wish to pursue the topic.

Professor Edward stood again, clutching a big key that looked as if it might have been forged for some medieval dungeon, and unlocked a wooden chest shoehorned in among several piles of books against one wall. He came back with a dozen or so thick manila folders containing papers of various sizes and quality. Some appeared to be of good rag, others of brittle pulp. "W. G. F. Smith's papers," he announced. "I don't know

The Colonel's Daughter

why I have clung so tightly to them, Mr. Hawkins, but now, with my own mortality in sight, perhaps it is time to turn them out to the world. You may, if you like, read them. And if the knowledge contained here helps prevent another colossal miscarriage of history such as that scoundrel Oliver Wiggins has foisted upon the world, historians will be the better for it.

The old Professor returned to his chair, a curiously serene look upon his worn face. My face was anything but serene, for I had found exactly what I had come in search of! And secretly, I believed, so had Professor Thomas Edward.

Chapter One

Colonel Willard Holmes raised a hand and at once the two men riding behind him drew rein. Holmes glanced back at them. *Old habits die hard*, he thought somberly, and he might have grinned if this mission hadn't been so serious, or his spirits so deeply mired in fear and dread.

"What is it, Colonel?" asked Caleb Cross, a wiry man in a corduroy coat.

Holmes was a tall, gray-haired man, still fit at nearly sixty years old. He had fought in the War of 1812, but had retired from Old Hickory's army after driving the British from New Orleans nearly nineteen years ago. Yet even after all these years, Caleb Cross and others still called him "Colonel."

Holmes peered out across the rolling grass prairie at the thread of gray smoke rising in the still air. "Over there," he said.

Chester Hampstead, a stocky, barrel-chested bull-whacker by profession, and a one-time sergeant under

The Colonel's Daughter

Holmes's command in another time and another life, squinted hard against the harsh light where the brilliant blue sky came down to touch the ridge of spring-green prairie grass. "I see it. A campfire?"

"Chimney smoke I think," Holmes said, getting his horse moving. They bounded up the rolling land and, cresting the ridge, halted their horses and looked down on a small building, half dug into a hillside near a creek. A couple of Indian ponies were tied to a hitching post out front where a short, bearded man with a sunburned head was hauling down on the long handle of a skin press. As Holmes and his friends rode in, the man turned the job of pressing the buffalo hides over to a Sioux warrior nearby and came over.

"You three look like you've been doing some pretty hard riding," the man said with a French accent. "Step down off those horses and have a drink." He sleeved the sweat from his brow and patted it from his head, then strode to a water barrel buried in the ground, in the shade of the building.

Holmes, Cross, and Hampstead followed him and drank deeply of the cool water.

"What is this place?" Holmes asked.

"It's the Bordeaux Trading Post, and that down there is Bordeaux Creek."

"And you?" Holmes inquired.

"James Bordeaux." He grinned. "Where you three headed? Got a good stock of Dupont and galena, baca too, if you need it. Got blankets and tinware as well, although you boys look pretty well outfitted."

"Don't need anything, thanks, except some information."

Bordeaux scratched his bald head. "Don't have much of that, sorry."

"I'm looking for a girl—"

"I'd like one of them myself."

Holmes shot him an impatient look. "The girl I'm looking for is my daughter."

Doug Hawkins

Bordeaux wiped the grin from his face, seeing the sudden fire that burned in the tall man's narrow, blue eyes. "How can I help you with that?"

"She was taken from her home in Independence last fall. There were four of them. Trappers heading west; they told me as much when they bought supplies from our store. One of them took a shine to my daughter, and when she gave him a cold shoulder, he kidnapped her." There was a catch in Holmes's voice. "Took her practically from right under our noses, and we never knew it until morning. By then they had a good head start. One that I still haven't been able to close . . . even after all these months," Holmes added bitterly.

"I've seen lots of trappers come through here, mister, but I don't recollect seeing any women—not any white women, at least."

Once again Holmes felt the fragile framework of his hopes begin to crumble. It had been the same story he'd heard everywhere they had stopped these long eight months. His hopes of ever finding his daughter alive were quickly fading. He had even considered giving up on the search—but not just yet!

"What were the names of the men what took your girl, mister?"

The frown on Holmes's weathered face deepened. "I don't know that, Mr. Bordeaux. They never gave their names . . . and afterwards I could find no one who knew them."

Bordeaux shook his head as if he too realized the hopelessness of the quest in a land as vast as this. "Sorry I can't help, but I'll keep an eye out for your daughter."

Holmes went to his horse and came back carrying a leather case. He worked the buckles, and withdrew a small, framed portrait. "This is what she looks like. It's . . ." again his voice almost cracked under the strain, "it's the only rendering of her I have."

Bordeaux studied the painting closely. "She's a pretty

girl. If I see her, I'll do what I can, mister. What's her name?"

"Marjory. Marjory Holmes."

Bordeaux returned the picture to the Colonel. "I wish you the best of luck." Then something occurred to him. "Say, Captain William Sublette is building a trading post at the confluence of the Laramie and North Platte Rivers. It's called Fort William. At one time or another Sublette has trapped or traded with most every man working these Rocky Mountains. You might see if he knows anything."

Holmes carefully returned the portrait to its leather case, fastened the lid down over it. "Thank you for your help, Mr. Bordeaux."

"Wish I had the words you were looking to hear, Colonel."

The three man-hunters swung back onto their horses, and turned them to the southwest, and Fort William.

Easing through the tall-pine forest, Kit Carson's moccasined feet made no sound as he emerged at the edge of a clearing, green with new spring grass, yet mottled here and there by patches of last winter's snow in the shade of towering fir and quaking aspen. Kit's swift glance took in every detail of the little glade, then narrowed sharply upon a smudge of brown half hidden among the clumps of serviceberry. A small grin worked its way across the mountain man's face. He had been tracking this quarry most of the last two hours, and now he had it in his sights!

Kit brought the long rifle to his shoulder, and as he steadied it, his finger reached for the trigger. The rifle boomed and the next instant a massive bull elk crashed through the undergrowth. The animal bounded up toward the rim of the glade, stumbled, and went to his knees. Scrambling, the wounded animal regained his feet, took a half dozen steps, then stumbled again and went down hard.

Doug Hawkins

Kit charged out of cover, the fringe of his buckskin shirt flying as he raced across the moist grass toward the wounded animal. They would have fresh meat in camp tonight, he was thinking, caught up in the excitement of the hunt and not paying attention to anything around him except the thrashing of the elk upon the ground. He yanked the butcher knife from his belt as he dropped to his knees, and setting the rifle aside, he went to work, first slitting the thick-muscled throat and putting the animal out of its suffering.

Kit was not a large man, but his hard muscles and quick wit made him a match for any man or beast. Just the same, there was more meat here than he could possibly carry back to camp, so he concentrated on quartering the elk. The heavy rear haunch would make fine dining for the ten trappers he was traveling with.

Kit had started out the previous fall from Taos with Captain Lee, trapping and trading goods to the men of the mountains. After over-wintering with Mr. Robidoux and his company at the mouth of the Winty River, Kit was restless to be on the move again. He had heard that Major Fitzpatrick and Jim Bridger were trapping down along the Snake River. He and some friends decided to join up with Fitzpatrick, but that crowded the countryside a bit too much for Kit's liking, as Fitzpatrick already had about thirty men working for him. Kit and his two partners, Bull Jackson and Ozzie Warner, left the company, heading for the Laramie River, intending to trap along the way, and eventually meet up with Captain William Sublette at the junction of the Laramie and North Platte Rivers, where Sublette was building his new outpost.

Along the way they had met a party of trappers led by a booshway named Gilbert McCaine. McCaine was a stocky, gray-eyed son of a Methodist preacher, and they threw in with him and his men, seeing as they were all heading more or less in the same direction. It was always safer traveling with a large company, especially

The Colonel's Daughter

in hostile Indian country. This part of the Rocky Mountains, however, was mostly inhabited by the Utah Indians. The Utes, as they were called, were horse thieves, to be sure, and they'd steal the clothes off your back given half a chance, but to Kit's knowledge, they weren't particularly hostile.

Kit worked at parting the elk meat, concentrating on the task . . . concentrating perhaps too much, he decided later when he had a moment to think back on what happened next. In a nearby thicket came a soft rustling sound. At first Kit dismissed it as leaves shifting on the breeze. Only, there was no breeze. Kit's blade stopped working. There it was again. He glanced quickly over his shoulder, and at that moment two grizzly bears pushed through the thick growth, their noses tilted high, sniffing the air to beat the band. They'd caught the elk's blood scent, and were nearly upon Kit and his kill.

Now, Kit knew that when God handed out eyes, the bear was at the tail end of that line, so these two might not even have seen him if he didn't twitch a muscle. But their noses—that was another story! Even if these two couldn't quite spy him out, they'd for certain *smell* him out!

The bears paused, tasting the air again, then lowering their massive heads. Tiny brown eyes straining and the silver tips of their fur shining in the sunlight, they broke into a shambling gait; huge paws reaching out and pounding the ground, enormous shoulders rolling beneath rippling fur and muscles. The roar that issued forth fairly shook the ground.

Fleeing from a pair of grizzlies is akin to waving a red cloth before a snorting bull, but these two bruins were coming on fast, and Kit didn't cotton to the looks they were giving him. Leaping to his feet, he grabbed up his rifle from the grass and dashed away. He hadn't bothered to reload the rifle after making his kill, but even if he had, it would have done him little good. One

Doug Hawkins

shot between two grizzlies, even to Kit, who had
shunned schooling, still ciphered out to one dead
hunter.

The grizzlies stopped short, nearly as startled to see
Kit springing into a run as Kit had been at discovering
them. It took them a moment to decide what to do
about it, and when they had, they broke into hot pursuit
as if suddenly spurred by a swarm of mad hornets.

Kit put on a burst of speed, but he was no match for
a pair of charging bears, even under the best of conditions, and this tall, damp grass, littered with hidden
twigs that seemed to reach out and grab at his moccasins, was anything but the best of conditions. A glance
over his shoulder made Kit's blood run cold. He threw
down the useless rifle and swerved for the nearest tree,
a half heartbeat ahead of the grizzlies. With the devil
breathing down his neck, he leaped for a branch, swung
his legs up onto another, and lifted his rear end an instant before a swiping claw lashed out at him, brushing
the seat of his britches, and then he was scrambling up
the branches like a scared monkey. He climbed as high
as he could before the tree began to bend under his
weight and he backed off a few feet, finding a secure
perch about fifteen feet above the ground.

Fur and fury flew below. The bears in their frustra-
tion began uprooting smaller trees, and attacked the
full-grown aspen wherein Kit had found sanctuary. The
aspen shuddered under the bruins' repeated blows, but
it stood solid; more than a match for the grizzlies.

After Kit's heart slowed, and the fire of breathing left
his throat, he settled down to watch the spectacle below. "I've got all day, boys," Kit said easily, grinning
now. "You keep that up and you'll likely knock yourself
silly."

As if it understood, one of the grizzlies turned from
the tree and lumbered back to the elk for a leisurely
lunch. The other, however, was not so easily put off.

Kit kept a tight grip as the tree shook beneath the

bear's violent attack and he wondered how long he'd have to remain up here. He'd heard tales of men being run up a tree by bears and kept there for days. Kit glanced at the elk across the way and his stomach growled. He'd been without food since breakfast, more than nine hours ago.

It was embarrassing to be treed by these critters, but at least none of his buddies was around to witness the disgrace. Kit had been run up and down the countryside by Indians on various occasions, and was even chased off by an irate badger once, when he had been eight or ten. But this was the first time ever that he'd been treed like a coon. After a while, Kit took a plug of tobacco from his hunting pouch and bit off a piece of it. He'd have preferred a smoke, but had no way of making fire, clinging as he was to the branches of the tree. When he had worked the chaw down some and had a mouthful of spit, he took aim and splattered the bear across its broad forehead. The grizzly roared in his fury and Kit laughed heartily.

"Got you that time, son!" he said with a grin, working up a second mouthful of tobacco juice. Filling his cheeks, he scored another direct hit.

That only seemed to infuriate the bear more, and he tramped around the tree as if studying the problem. Kit settled down to wait him out. The sun was warm upon his face, and come summer his sunburned skin would break out in a rash of freckles which was always a vexation to him, but it was something he couldn't help. And no man had better make a remark about it!

The bear was a persistent beast, while across the glade, his companion had completely forgotten the incident and was happily feeding himself from Kit's elk. That rankled Kit some, but there was little he could do about it. He spied his rifle a ways off, laying in the grass, and made a mental note that the next time he went hunting he would make certain the piece was reloaded before he claimed his kill.

Doug Hawkins

Below, the bear bellowed with rage, shook his head, and ran a few paces out into the glade. He stopped, shook his head, then charged back, slamming his broad shoulder into the tree trunk. The concussion nearly knocked Kit from his perch.

Finally the bear gave up and lumbered across the glade to his companion. He shoved his huge muzzle into the carcass and went to work on what was left of the elk. Just the same, Kit was still up the tree, and now all he could do was watch until the grizzlies decided to leave. He was about to settle down for what might prove to be a long wait when a flash of light off the nearby ridge caught his eye. He peered at the rocky ridge, wondering what it was.

There it was again. Then it was gone.

After a few minutes Kit had figured out that if he shifted his position along the branch, he'd catch another glimpse of that strange flash of light. The afternoon wore on, and as the sun moved across the sky, so did that odd glimmer in the distance. By late noon Kit had shinnied out onto the branch as far as his weight would permit before the shimmering finally vanished altogether. The sun had moved too far to the west.

It got his curiosity up, and in pondering the meaning of the strange flash of light, Kit practically forgot about the two bears feasting on his elk only a few hundred feet away.

Chapter Two

It was nearly dusk before the bears finally had their fill of the elk and wandered off. Kit gave them enough time to be well away, then climbed down and retrieved his rifle. He loaded the piece immediately, and with the solid reassurance of the heavy, 32-gauge J. J. Henry in his hand once again, he gave in to his curiosity and made his way up the slope to the ridge where he had tracked the flash of light throughout the afternoon.

Having fixed the spot in his brain, it took only a few moments to line up the landmarks. The area was a rocky outcropping, and when at first Kit didn't discover anything unusual, he suspected that the flash might have come from an outcropping of mica. He searched a little while longer, but the sun was sinking lower toward the horizon, and he was about to give up and return to camp. Then he spied it.

Curious, he thought, hunkering down. A mirror . . . but not like any mirror he had ever seen in these parts before. It was a lady's hand mirror, much like one that his half sister Sophia owned. Only this one was made of silver and polished wood, and inlayed with what appeared to be the polished bits and pieces of a seashell. He reached to pick it up, then stopped. Even more curious than it being here was the *way* it was here. It hadn't been dropped as if accidentally lost. It had been *placed*! Its slant seemed to have been carefully calculated. The mirror was anchored in place with some rocks, and a twig kept it tilted back at precisely the angle at which whoever had set it there wished to keep it.

Kit had never encountered such a thing in the wilderness. Who, he wondered, could have set it up? And why? He placed his head low, and sighted along the path that a beam of sunlight might take if reflected off the polished face. It would vary according to the time of day, of course, and even the time of year, but maybe, just maybe . . .

In the distance he spied the flicker of a campfire far down the side of the mountain, along the trail they had been following. Upon studying the matter further, he realized the fire was from the trappers' camp that he was a part of. He sat up, puzzlement scrunching up his lips, then removed the mirror from its perch. Turning it over, Kit saw that the shell inlays on the back of it formed letters . . . and that the letters made up two words . . .

He frowned as the swift, heavy hand of inadequacy pressed down upon him—it happened whenever he was confronted with the dilemma of reading. Although he did not admit it freely, Kit Carson couldn't read half a sentence, couldn't even write his own name.

The mirror was a puzzle, and Kit didn't mind a puzzle or two, so long as he was able to work out the solution in the end. He put the mirror in his hunting bag, and grabbing up the long rifle, started back to camp.

Kit smelled the fire and heard the voices a long way back.

The Colonel's Daughter

"Hail the camp!" he called while still several dozen feet away. It was a precaution they all took. A bit of a warning to those men sitting around the fire precluded being greeted by half a dozen musket balls.

"That you, Kit?" McCaine called out. McCaine was the booshway, the leader of these trappers, and it was his place to take charge.

"It is," Kit said, emerging from the deep blackness of the forest now that night had come upon the mountain.

William "Bull" Jackson, a huge, thick-necked man with a massive black beard and broad shoulders, had been Kit's traveling companion since they both left Taos with Captain Lee the previous fall. In spite of the man's immense, ungainly appearance—like the creature from which he had taken his nickname—Bull was a man of book-learning and refined manners, Beyond that, Kit knew little of his past. Bull had been sitting near the fire reading a book when Kit came in. He usually read in the evenings; sometimes from Shakespeare, and sometimes from the Bible, often entertaining the men with the stories. Now Bull lowered the book and said, "Where's all that venison you said you'd be toting back, Kit? Don't tell me you left it for us to fetch."

Ozzie Warner said, "Don't you know it's uncivil to ask that of a man who comes into camp empty-handed?" They had spent winter quarters together with Robidoux, and the gray-bearded trapper whose cheeks seemed always aglow had come along with Kit and Bull when they had pulled out.

Bull smirked at Ozzie and said, "Give thy thoughts no tongue, Nor any unproportioned thought his act. Be thou familiar but by no means vulgar."

As usual, when Bull yanked a line like that from Shakespeare and cast it out at them, they all just stared blankly for a moment then shook their heads. Bull laughed at his own private joke.

"I was starting to wonder where you had gotten to," McCaine said.

Doug Hawkins

"I could sure use a cup of that thar coffee," Kit replied, setting his rifle against a tree and taking a tin cup from his possibles bag. He poured himself some, then settled down, cross-legged, out of the glow of the fire, and warmed his hands around the cup. "I got me an elk, all right," he said after a few minutes. "Tracked the critter most all morning and part of the afternoon, then I made a clean kill. Only problem was, a couple grizzly bears showed up and decided I ought to share it with them."

"Is that a fact?" Bull said skeptically, but with an amiable chuckle that might have passed for a minor earthquake.

"It is," Kit said unruffled. "You know me, I don't stretch a story six ways to Sunday like some of you boys."

They laughed.

"We tussled some over the decision, but seeing as there was two of them and only one of me, I relinquished my claim and climbed up into the branches of a tree to wait until they had taken their fill and gone on their way. By that time, there warn't much left of my elk."

"So you come back empty-handed."

"Not exactly." Kit took the mirror from his hunting bag and handed it across to Bull. The trappers gathered around to look at it. "I found that propped up on the side of a hill. What do you make of it?"

"What in the devil is a fancy thing like that doing way the hell out here?" a trapper by the name of Filby asked.

"That's sort of the same question I asked myself. Thar's a word or two on the back of it."

Bull turned the mirror over. "It's a name," he said. "Marjory Holmes."

"That's curious." McCaine took the mirror and studied it. "Wonder how it come to be here."

"It's plain enough," Ozzie Warner said. "It belongs to

26

a white woman, but there ain't many white women in a place like this."

"I'd sure take notice if I'd seen one," Kit said, grinning. The men chuckled and agreed that a white woman would be quite a sight in these parts. About all they ever met were Indian women. On a rare occasion a white woman might show up at a rendezvous—but always with a husband, and maybe a child or two; passing through on their way to the trading posts or to missions in Oregon.

McCaine gave the mirror back to Kit. "You keep it handy. Maybe someday you'll find yourself a little Injun gal and make her a present of it."

It was a nicely made mirror; a possession Kit felt a woman would surely treasure. He imagined that it might have been a gift at one time. Certainly, it was a thing she would not casually leave behind. "I'll keep it all right," Kit said, putting it away, "but I intend to give it back to the woman who lost it."

The mirror was mostly forgotten the next morning as they loaded their beaver pelts onto the pack horses and started along the mountain trail. It was a path well traveled, and Kit figured that once Sublette's new fort was completed, the Laramie Trace would become a busy thoroughfare, connecting the open grasslands to the east of the Rocky Mountains with the rich beaver country to the west. Towering pine trees crowded near the trail as they rode, and the spring air was heavily perfumed with pine needles that blanketed the moist forest floor, warmed by a high sun. It was a pretty countryside, but Kit felt a longing for Taos, down in Mexico, where he had been living the last several years. He'd grown fond of the easy life there; the quaint adobe homes that seemed to be one with the brown earth, the temperate winters, and, of course, the pretty señoritas.

"Look there, Kit," Bull said, yanking Kit from his pleasant reverie. The big man was pointing ahead where the trace they were following took a fork. Kit tapped his horse's flanks and galloped ahead. By the time the others arrived, Kit had reached up into the branches overhanging the trail and was pulling down something fastened to a long, leather thong. The men circled around him.

McCaine leaned forward in his saddle. "What did you find there?"

"Looks to be a lady's hair comb." Kit removed the mirror from his bag and compared the two items. "What do you make of this? A matched set."

"If that ain't the queerest thing I ever did see," Ozzie said, scratching his head.

Kit's eyes narrowed thoughtfully. "It's plain this was put here just so someone passing by would find it."

"But by who?" a trapper named Grove asked, and not surprisingly, it was the very question that was on each of their minds.

"I don't know," Kit said, "But I have a mighty uneasy feeling about this."

"Me too," Bull rumbled. "You don't suppose some white gal went and got herself took by Injuns, do you, Kit?"

Kit shoved the comb and the mirror back into his hunting bag and looked around. "The trace forks here. I wonder . . ." He let the thought trail off, unfinished.

"This way will take us down to Sublette's fort," McCaine said, nodding his head towards the east fork.

"Maybe, but I think I'll ride along this one for a while." Kit grinned. "Who knows, I might find me a brush or some hairpins along the way."

McCaine frowned. "Well, it is a damned peculiar thing. I reckon it won't hurt none to ride along with you a piece, Kit. I'm curious to get to the bottom of this myself."

The trappers spent the morning scouring the trail for more signs, but by noon had discovered nothing. They had proposed a dozen different explanations for the comb and mirror, had rejected nearly as many, and kept coming back to the same conclusion: A white girl must have been kidnapped by Indians. When noon came and went, Kit began to think they'd never get to the bottom of the mystery, and that maybe they should turn back and resume their journey to Fort William.

One thing bothered Kit about the kidnapping theory. That whole morning he'd not seen a single hoof print, or any other Indian sign. . . . Suddenly he drew up.

"What is it?" Bull asked.

Kit sniffed the slight breeze. "Smoke. Thar's a fire up ahead."

The others smelled it too.

"Injuns!" McCaine growled.

Checking their rifles, they slipped lightly off their mounts. After handing the reins over to Filby to hold, the company of mountain men advanced the rest of the way on foot.

Seth Wilson strode up from the river toward the little cabin, his buckskin pants soaked to the thighs, four St. Louis pattern beaver traps slung over his shoulder, and a Lehman rifle at his side in his right hand. He was in a foul mood as he tramped towards the cabin, where a curl of smoke from the chimney at least held out the promise of a cup of hot coffee. He'd lost two traps that morning, and the other six had been sprung, but were empty. The beaver had cleverly learned how to approach the castoreum-baited stick without springing the trap. "Beaver has gotten just too smart in these parts," he complained aloud to himself, and kicked a stone out of his path.

All at once he stopped, listening. Something was wrong. Something was terribly wrong, for the forest was suddenly dead silent. Dropping his traps, Wilson swung around, his rifle ready, and froze where he stood at what he saw.

Chapter Three

Kit Carson had an impulsive streak running through him that had gotten him in trouble more than once, but it had also pulled his bacon from the frying pan a time or two when cool logic suggested one thing, but his spontaneity had propelled him to do the opposite. That he was one of the best scouts in the mountains was undisputed, so now he took the lead as the mountain men left the trace behind and sliced silently through the tall trees. Bull and Ozzie stuck near their partner while McCaine ordered his men to fan out in a wide arch that stretched more than a dozen rods along the climbing land.

The odor of smoke grew stronger as Kit edged up toward the crest of the hill. Silently, he gave a hand signal to Bull and Ozzie. The two men moved off a few feet to either side of him and inched up to the rim until they could look down the other side.

Kit watched a man emerge from the stream below the rude cabin, and it was plain by his belligerent strides that he was infuriated over something. As the others reached the crest of the hill, staying low, Kit took in the lay of the homestead below. There was a lean-to corral nearby, empty at the moment. Six hobbled horses grazed in a grassy swell that ran down to the river. The smoke he had smelled was coming from a crude wattle and daub chimney. The cabin had one window; no glass, just an oilcloth curtain. As he studied the place, he caught a glimpse of movement past the curtain.

McCaine came along the back of the ridge, bent low. "What do you make of it?"

Kit eased back and sat up. "There's someone inside the cabin, probably armed. But I don't think they would be fool enough to start any trouble if we all drop in for a visit."

McCaine grinned. "That's about how I see it too. You make out a girl down there?"

"No, but I did see movement inside the cabin."

"Well, then let's go on down there and say hello."

And so this was why, when Seth Wilson had swung around with his rifle ready, he had stopped stone-still in his tracks with nine fierce mountain men and nine big-bore rifles staring back at him.

"Afternoon," Kit said amiably, coming forward a couple of steps, his J. J. Henry held low at his waist, casual-like, but with its front sight lined up on the man's navel.

"What do you want with me? I ain't got nothing worth stealing here."

"Steal? Why, that wouldn't be a neighborly thing to do, now would it, mister?" Kit said easily, and just to prove his good intentions, he shifted the muzzle of his rifle a trifle to the left of the man's belly button.

"Sneaking up on a fellow, armed to the teeth like you boys are, don't strike me as a neighborly thing either," he replied, but was clearly relieved that along with Kit's rifle, the other eight had strayed slightly from their intended mark as well. The man likewise lowered his smokepole.

"We smelled your cook fire," Kit said, "and got to wondering where it was coming from. My name is Carson, Christopher Carson, but folks just generally call me Kit."

"Seth Wilson," the other announced. "I'd offer you a cup of coffee, but we're plum out of the stuff. So, now that your curiosity has been sated, you can leave."

"*Sated?*" Windy Henderson hooted, "Woo-weee, that's a fancy word. What ever does it mean?"

Bull Jackson said, "It means the same as satisfied. Your curiosity has been satisfied."

"Well, why didn't he just say so?"

Kit grinned back at Wilson. "Who else is in that cabin?"

Wilson cast a quick glance at the cabin door. "Ain't no one here but me."

"Is that a fact? Then you won't mind me just taking a peek inside for myself?"

Wilson looked worried and chewed his lip while his eyes darted across the line of men behind Kit. "OK, there *is* someone else. It's my brother, Sam, and my boy, Billy. Bill ain't feeling too good, you see. That's why I told you I was alone." Wilson craned his head over his shoulder and called, "Sam . . . Sam, step out here, won't you? And bring Billy with you."

In a moment a young boy stepped tentatively from the door, wearing a wide look in his blue eyes that Kit judged to be fright. Right behind him came the boy's uncle. Sam Wilson was a beanpole of a man, whereas his brother, Seth, was built a little like a short version of Bull Jackson, all shoulders and not much neck. Sam had a short, red beard, red hair poking past the hat on his head, and odd green eyes that Kit found vaguely disturbing. Seth, Kit realized, wasn't much older than himself, although at first sight he had judged the man to be nearer to forty than thirty.

The Colonel's Daughter

Sam, on the other hand, was at least forty, mostly bald, with a smattering of gray among what was left of the red. Billy looked like neither of them, and Kit decided he had gotten the blue eyes and sandy hair from his mother.

"This here is Mr. Carson," Seth said, his voice tight and still a little nervous. "Billy, say howdy to the man."

Billy was wearing buckskin trousers and a baggy, red wool shirt that must have belonged to his father. He took a short, uncertain step forward and stopped abruptly, as if coming to attention, with his uncle crowding in right behind him. "Hello . . . hello, Mr. Carson," he said in the soft voice of a boy who had not yet become a man. Carson judged him to be about twelve or thirteen years old, at that tall and gangly stage of life.

He grinned at the lad. "Hello, Billy. No need to fret none, me and the boys here don't mean you or your pa no harm." Kit couldn't help but notice the ugly purple welt upon the boy's face. It might have been from the sickness Wilson said the boy had, but Kit rather suspected that he'd recently been struck by an open hand.

"I'm right pleased to have company—"

Sam Wilson dropped a hard hand upon the boy's shoulder and said, "You need to get back into bed. You ain't well enough yet to be up and visiting."

Billy must have had the ague right bad, Kit thought, for all at once the boy began to shiver. His uncle backed him into the cabin just then, his hand still firm upon his shoulder, and closed the door.

"There, that's all of us," Seth said, not near as nervous as he had been.

"Is it?" Kit glanced at the empty corral with its lean-to barn. "I see six horses over yonder, but you've got enough tack for twice that many."

Seth's anger boiled to the surface. "What I got ain't none of your business, Carson. Now, if you please, I'd

33

just as soon see you and your friends turn around and leave us be."

"Tell me, Mr. Wilson, what are you and your kin doing away out here?"

"Trapping. And now you can leave."

McCaine came over. "Prime beaver country hereabouts. How have your lines been running?"

"Who are you?"

"McCaine's my name. I'm the Booshway of this here party."

"You're their leader? I figured Carson here was."

"No, Mr. Carson and his friends only joined us on the trail a few weeks back."

Wilson shifted his attention from Kit. "Trapping's been fair enough. It was pretty good when we first come to this place last fall, but we've worked the streams steady and nearly got the lot of 'em. What's left has learned enough to not let themselves get caught. Reckon it's time to pull up stakes and move on."

"Yep. There comes a time to do that." McCaine glanced at the sky. "But then there comes a time to settle in too. Like right now. Almost too late for us to think about moving on. It will be dark in another hour or so. Good water here, good grazing for our animals too. I don't suppose you would mind if my boys set up camp over yonder. We won't be no bother to you, and come morning we'll be pulling out early."

Kit knew that McCaine had seen how it was going and had stepped in to smooth things over. McCaine could have a right silver tongue when the situation called for it, Kit mused, easing out of the conversation and going back to his friends.

"What's McCaine up to, Kit?" Ozzie Warner asked on the sly. "We have plenty of daylight left to make a good march."

"Buying us more time. We still haven't asked him about the girl, Marjory Holmes. And the way him and me was a-heading, he'd not have helped us even if he could."

"Think he knows anything?" Bull asked.

"Maybe . . . and maybe not. One thing for certain, he's lying about there being only the three of them. And another thing. That boy, Billy, he's scared to death of his father. That poor kid has been whaled into a time or two."

Ozzie gave a short laugh. "If Seth Wilson is anything like my pa was, I can understand why the kid is scared. I saw the bruise on Billy's face, and I can remember looking just like he looks more than once. Pa would just as soon whoop me as look at me, 'specially when he'd been drinking. I still carry the scars on my hinder side to prove it. That's why I let out of there when I was ten. And I ain't never been back since."

Kit said, "I run away too, when I was sixteen."

"Why did you take to the road?" Bull asked.

Kit got a far-off look in his eyes. "I'd been bound to a saddler named David Workman, as an apprentice to learn his trade. It would have been a good trade, too, but you see, I had me a bad case of wanderlust—still do. I couldn't see myself settling down in one place long enough to go into business, nor did I care about fixing someone else's leather goods for the rest of my life. So, I up and run away."

"Didn't they go looking for you?"

Kit smiled. "Why, sure they did. Ain't that what they're suppose to do? Workman even put a reward out for my return. All of one cent."

"One cent!" Bull roared, laughing. "He sure didn't want you back very badly, did he?"

A roguish glint came to Kit's eyes, then he gave a short laugh and lowered his voice conspiratorially. "The truth of the matter is, Workman had a touch of the wanderlust himself. We talked about the West a whole lot those two years that I worked for him. I desperately wanted to go, but my stepfather had bound me to Workman and wouldn't hear of it. Finally, when I made up my mind to leave, he agreed to put the hounds onto a cold trail. While I was heading south, he sent them north. In fact, less than a year later David Workman left Missouri for Santa Fe, where we later met up and toasted our good fortune."

"So, he was in on your escape all along," Ozzie said. "That's why he only offered one cent for your return. He didn't want nobody looking too seriously for you."

"He was, for a fact," Kit allowed, his attention divided, part of it on the conversation McCaine and Wilson were still having.

McCaine came over a few minutes later. "He says we can camp down by the river for tonight, but he wasn't too happy about it."

"After we get settled in, I'd say we bring Mr. Seth Wilson a peace offering."

"What do you have in mind, Kit?"

"Well, if he was an Injun, I'd take him some beads and brass bells. But seeing as he's not, I've still a little bit left in a jug that I bought from Captain Lee before his stock ran out."

McCaine's gray eyes widened. "You mean whiskey?"

"John Barleycorn's best. Back home we call it 'Taos Lightning.' "

"Why, Kit, if I'd known you was carrying whiskey I'd have arm-wrestled you out of it long before now."

"Now, what would your preacher pappy say if'n he heard you now?"

"He'd say I was a sinner a-going to hell. But I already knew that."

Darkness was upon the land and the waxing moon scattering its silvery light across the rippling water when Kit and McCaine strolled up from the camp and knocked on the cabin's door. It opened six inches and Seth Wilson's belligerent face poked out.

"What do you want?" he barked.

The Colonel's Daughter

"To show you how much we appreciated your hospitality, we figured on letting you share our good fortune." Kit held out the jug.

Wilson's disagreeableness mellowed some, and casting a quick glance over his shoulder into the dimly lit cabin, he slipped outside and immediately shut the door behind him. They walked off a few paces and sat upon a felled tree near the stream. The jug of Taos Lightning made its way between them.

"Nice place you got here," McCaine noted.

"It was OK for the winter."

"Sounds like you're fixing to leave?" Kit asked.

"The streams are about trapped out, and we got ourselves a cache of pelts that me and my partners need to sell."

"Partners? I thought it was just you and your brother."

"Oh, yeah. Well, him and my boy, I count them as partners seeing as they shared in the work."

"That sounds only fair," McCaine said.

"Damn right its fair," Wilson gruffed, appropriating the jug for another swallow.

Kit never much cared for small talk when he had pressing business on his mind, so he came right to the point. "You know anything about a white girl hereabouts?"

Wilson glanced over with a jerk that would have snapped his neck if he hadn't been built like Bull Jackson. "What are you driving at?" he asked, suspicion rising in his voice.

"We found a mirror along our back trail. There was a name on it: Marjory Holmes. We were wondering how it came to be way out here in the middle of God's creation, five hundred miles from the nearest civilized settlement. And you're the only one around to ask."

"I don't know nothing about no—" He stopped all at once as if a thought had suddenly occurred to him, then he said, "Wait a minute now. I did hear about a party

37

of trappers what come through these parts just before winter set in. Seems to me that there was a white woman with them."

"Where have they gone?"

"Gone? They're dead. All dead . . . except the girl. What I heard was . . ." He paused, toying with them like a man might with a playful cat, dangling a ball of yarn just out of its reach. "You know, my mouth is gettin' mighty dry."

Kit set the jug into his hands and waited while Wilson took his fill of it. When he handed it back, the jug was bone dry. Kit frowned and said, "Did that oil up your jaws any?"

"It did some. Now, like I was saying, I heard they was all killed, all but the girl. She was taken away by them Injuns."

"Who done it?" McCaine demanded. Wilson's stalling was rubbing a thin spot in his patience.

"It was the Utes. The ones with Walker."

"Utes?" Kit knew the Utah Indians. He had spent some time in Chief Walkara's village the previous spring. "The Utes are horse thieves, not women stealers. Anyway, they've not proven hostile to any trappers I've ever talked to."

"That's your opinion, mister," Wilson shot back. "They come sneaking 'round here all the time. Nowadays whenever one of them groveling savages gets too close to my place I shoot first and palaver second."

The discussion ended with that and Wilson stood abruptly and marched into his cabin, loudly dropping the bolt on the other side of the door to lock it. McCaine and Kit glanced at each other. McCaine said, "If the Utes have become hostile in these parts, it's easy to see why."

Kit stared at the beaten-silver track of water beneath the moonlight. "Ain't many men I take to distrusting right off, Gilbert, but that Seth Wilson, he comes closest to any that I can remember."

The Colonel's Daughter

They started back to camp. "You think he's talking straight, Kit?"

The rippling surface of the water looked like a million chips of broken glass flowing across the land; a pretty sight against the tall, dark pine trees. A man with nothing much to do might spend considerable time sitting and smoking a pipe of tobacco, watching the river's hypnotic ways. There was the whisper of wind in the treetops, and the chill spring night had turned their breath into faint gray puffs of steam.

Kit frowned. "I'm certain he's hiding something." They had begun to walk again.

McCaine gave a short laugh. "Half the men in the West are hiding something, Kit. You know that. They've done something back east and the law, or family, got too hot for them. The only place wide-open enough to take them without asking questions is this wild country. A country filled with men like you and me."

"Oh, and what is it you're running from?" Kit asked.

McCaine grinned and said, "My pa, I reckon."

"He treat you poorly?"

"No, nothing like that. He was a stern man, and I'd seen the willow switch a time or two, but he wasn't mean about it. No, it was his hellfire and brimstone that finally drove me out. That, and his sense of righteousness which didn't exactly square with my own. You see, when I was about sixteen I got introduced to liquor and women, and kinda liked what I had found. Got to keeping regular company with both of them and he told me I was hell-bound for sure, but I didn't see where I was doing anything that warranted such a stiff indictment." McCaine paused and made a wry grin. "There was this pretty little gal up the road, and when she come to be in a family way and put the finger on me, Pa said I'd have to go and do the right thing by her and marry the girl. That was when I figured it was time to head west. Ain't been back since."

"Most men got something they keep hidden away,

Gilbert. I run away from home when I was sixteen, and Ozzie, he left when he was even younger than that. Then there's Bull—"

"Kind of a quiet man, ain't he? Always got his nose buried in a book," McCaine said.

"I've been traveling with Bull for eight months now, and I still don't know anything about him except that he came from Virginia."

"Virginia's a good place to be from. 'Mother of Presidents,' some call her. That's the nice thing about this life, Kit. You can come out here and leave your past back wherever it is you hail from, and no one is gonna pry too closely into it."

"I reckon so, Gilbert. But that still don't make folks like Mr. Seth Wilson any more easy to swallow."

Chapter Four

The men had built a big fire that sent sparks high into the sky. It was so bright that almost at once Kit and McCaine lost their night vision and the shadowy landscape around them faded into indistinguishable blackness. Kit cut a piece of meat from the roasting venison one of the trappers had shot earlier, and poured some coffee into his tin cup.

"Did you talk to the boy?" Ozzie asked.

"No, he didn't come out," Kit said. "Wilson keeps him locked up tighter than a parson's liquor chest."

Ozzie chuckled and shook his head. "I feel sorry for the kid. You know, if I get a chance before we pull out of here, I'm going to talk to him. If'n his pa is beating him like mine did to me, I can at least tell him what I done about it. He's as old as I was when I left home."

"You might not want to let Seth find out about it," Kit advised him. "That man's about a squirrelly as a keg of Dupont in a blacksmith's shop."

Ozzie laughed. "I've handled men like him before. Seth Wilson don't scare me."

Bull lowered the book that he'd been reading by fire-light and said, "Cowards die many times before their deaths; The valiant never taste of death but once."

For an instant you could hear a leaf fall. Then almost as if on cue, each groaned and shook his head. Bull chuckled and said, "What about the girl? Has he heard anything?"

"He heard a rumor about a white girl being held by the Utes."

"The Utes?" Bull scoffed. "Do you believe him?"

McCaine said, "It's possible, but I'd like to hear it from someone else before I go off on a search that might only lead in circles. Seth Wilson doesn't exactly inspire me with confidence."

Kit pondered that a moment. "If there's even a chance his story might be true, then someone needs to go and check it out."

Bull gave a short laugh. "I've heard that tone of voice before. It usually means we're in for another one of your adventures."

Kit grinned. "You don't have to come along. I'll go by myself."

"That's unlikely," Bull snorted. "A scrawny fellow like you needs someone to look after him."

Ozzie Warner pulled a burning twig from the fire and put it to the clay bowl of his pipe. "What will we do with our pelts, Kit? I'd hate to get into an Injun scuffle and lose 'em."

"We? You coming along too?"

"Shoot, Kit, I rode with the two of you all the way from the Snake River. I reckon I'll go along on this trip as well. Civilization and Bill Sublette's expensive whis-key will keep a little while longer. But I do worry about them goods we're carrying. Hate to see all my winter misery go for naught because we got careless and lost the pack animals chasing Ute Injuns up and down these mountains."

McCaine said, "Kit, you and your partners can have

The Colonel's Daughter

your gallivant. As for me, in the morning I'll be taking my boys' on down to Fort William like we planned. If you want, I'll haul your furs with me and leave them at the fort. You can settle with the company when you get back."

In the few weeks that they had traveled together, Kit had come to know Gilbert McCaine as an honest and reliable man. "That will be all right by me," he said, glancing at his friends to see how they would answer. Bull and Ozzie agreed to the arrangement, and it was settled. Come morning, McCaine and his group would resume their journey, and Kit with his partners would go and find themselves some Indians, and hopefully a white girl in need of rescuing.

With the coming of dawn, Kit loaded their furs upon three pack horses and put them in the care of Gilbert McCaine. McCaine extended a hand to Kit. "It's been a pleasure riding with you and your friends. I wish you luck on your endeavor."

He had a strong, sincere grip. Kit appreciated that. It was a sign of open honesty which he valued in a man. "I don't expect it will be more than a couple weeks. Maybe you and your men will still be at Fort William when we get back."

"If not, then we'll see you at the rendezvous on Ham's Fork this June."

"I plan to be there." Kit stepped back and Gilbert McCaine got his company moving. The trappers moved onto a trail that took them up and over the ridge where they had first spied Wilson's cabin the day before. The last of the pack horses, and then the "little Booshway" who rode rear guard, melted into the deep shadows that still clung close to the ground beneath the trees. When the party had finally dipped down over the other side, Kit turned back to his friends.

"Let's saddle up, boys. Don't want to let the sun find us napping." Once freed from the burden of the pack horses, Kit and his partners could cover a lot of miles, so long as they got an early start. The sky was brightening to the east, just beginning to turn the clouds a rosy hue.

Seth Wilson and his brother, Sam, left the cabin, glared at Kit and his partners, then strode down to the creek to check their trap lines.

Bull came up alongside Kit, towering over him a good dozen inches, his shoulders wider than a burlap sack of turnips. "There goes two of the most contentious men I have ever had the misfortune of meeting."

Kit rolled his shoulders beneath the colorful wool poncho that he wore to fend off the morning chill. He'd made the happy acquaintance with "ponchos" when he first came to Santa Fe in 1826 with a wagon train of trade goods. After trying one out for a few days, he decided that the peculiar Mexican article of clothing had a lot to recommend it, especially on chilly mornings like this. It offered warmth, protection from wind, and even kept him dry in a light drizzles, and it still left his arms free to move at an instant's notice.

"A certain amount of caution is a good thing when you live alone in the wilderness. But there is something to be said for being neighborly as well." Kit gave a small frown. "I reckon some men just don't know where the one leaves off and the other begins."

They watched Seth and Sam disappear around a bend in the stream where the forest grew thick and dark. "I won't miss his company none," Bull said, hefting his saddle onto his horse as if the thing had weighed no more than a table doily.

Kit tightened the cinches on his saddle and tied his bedroll behind it. He was just as eager to be away from the unpleasant pair as his partners were. The cabin door creaked softly and when Kit looked over, Billy Wilson was standing near the door, peering across the grassy meadow at them. The boy remained there a moment, as if not certain which way to step next, and even at this distance, Kit could see the fear that pulled at his young features. He glanced quickly toward the stream where the two men had gone, and not seeing Seth and Sam anywhere nearby, Billy started forward. He stopped all at once, as if suddenly changing his mind, turned away, and hurried into the forest behind the cabin.

"What do you make of that?" Bull asked, looking over the top of his saddle.

Kit frowned. "I don't know, but if that warn't a plea for help, I'll eat this here saddle—buckles and all." Kit handed his reins over to Bull. "Maybe I ought to go talk to the boy before we leave."

"No, let me do it," Ozzie said. "If Billy's having the sort of trouble I think he is, then talking to someone who's been through it too might help him."

"All right, go see what you can do. Only, be careful that Seth Wilson doesn't find you out, and don't take too long. I've got a real strong urge to see this valley over my shoulder."

Ozzie Warner grabbed up his long rifle and started across the meadow. The last that Kit saw of the lanky trapper was his ambling, bowlegged gait carrying him into the shadows of the trees behind the cabin.

Captain William Sublette frowned at the men standing across the spindly camp desk, which had been temporarily set up in the still incomplete log building that was supposed to be the fort's headquarters, and Sublette's office. "I'm sorry, Colonel, but I've not heard any word of a white girl in these parts. And the descriptions you've given of the men who took her—well, they could fit a half a hundred Rocky Mountain boys." Sublette looked back at portrait in his hands, then returned it to Colonel Holmes. "She's a lovely girl. I hope you find her."

"I will," Holmes said with quiet confidence and iron resolution . . . the same determination that had brought him and his fighting men successfully through the Battle of New Orleans; an unshakable resolve that had driven him on in the face of overwhelming military might to expel the British from American soil nearly twenty years earlier.

Sublette stood and accompanied the men out into the compound of the new fort, where newly arrived crates of trade goods sat under tarps, waiting for the store-rooms to be finished. The fort's log walls were not yet fully erected, and a gaping hole pierced them where soon a solid gate would stand as a first-line defense against the Sioux, Crow, Arapaho, and Cheyenne, if they should ever want to become hostile to the Company. Fort William was to be a trading post, not a military garrison—but hundreds of miles from civilization, trading posts were often built like military compounds.

Below lay the Laramie River, nearly hidden behind the thicket of cottonwood trees that crowded along its banks. As the men walked toward their horses, Chester Hampstead asked, "If it was you, Captain Sublette, where would you begin looking?"

"If it were I, Mr. Hampstead, I would go to the Rocky Mountain boys and ask them."

"And where might we find these men?" Caleb Cross inquired, pale blue eyes probing earnestly from the long, drawn face.

William Sublette swung an arm out in a arc that included everything laying to the south, west, and north of the fort. "They're all out there, sir, scattered around in over fifty thousand square miles of wild mountains and burning deserts. A land both wonderful and horrible; filled with Indians, bears, mountain lions, unbearable cold in the winter, and hoards of voracious black flies in the summer. The men who can help you are out there, Mr. Cross."

"How would you suggest we find these 'Rocky Mountain boys?'" Colonel Holmes asked.

The Colonel's Daughter

Sublette walked them beyond the half-finished walls of the fort to a knoll of high ground nearby. Around them rolling grassland stretched away in all directions. To the south, Holmes stared at a vast sea of buffalo grazing the unbroken country. From here they observed that the Laramie River was a wide, meandering river, broken up with many islands, each heavily forested. It merged with the North Platte about a mile and a half away.

"The Laramie River cuts up into the mountains directly to the west of us, and is a passage that trappers use frequently. If you go that way, you're likely to run into a party coming out of their winter quarters. That other river, the Platte, runs more to the north. It will take you around the mountains to South Pass, beyond which you will come upon the Snake River. I know that both Bridger and Fitzpatrick are working the Snake."

"Which would you take?"

"Hard to say. Both are good. Up the Laramie River you're likely to encounter the Ute Indians, and generally they leave you alone if you don't bother them. The other way is through the heart of the Arapaho, Sioux, Crow, Cheyenne . . . all fierce warriors and I'd not like to meet up with them myself, especially if I was traveling in a party only three men strong. But, you're going to have to make that choice yourself."

They returned to the fort, and as Holmes and his companions swung back onto their horses, Sublette said, "Here's another idea you might want to consider. The end of June is the time of this year's rendezvous. It will be at Ham's Fork of the Green River. You show up there and you'll have most every man in the area to talk to. One of them is bound to know of the men you're looking for—that is, if they're still in the mountains."

"You think they might not be?"

Sublette shook his head. "I can't know that, Colonel Holmes. But there is regular traffic all up and down the eastern slope of the Rocky Mountains. A man making it this far could easily turn south and end up in Santa Fe or Taos, or he might push right on through to Oregon and California."

Holmes frowned as his hopes sank further into the mire of despair. "What you're saying then is that my search is a hopeless waste of time."

"You're wrong, Colonel. I would never tell a father that his search for a lost child is a hopeless waste of time. My prayers go with you, sir. Good luck."

Colonel Holmes, Caleb Cross, and Chester Hampstead rode away from the fort and at the bank of the Laramie River the Colonel reined up.

"Which way, Colonel?" Cross asked, his thin frame leaning forward slightly in the saddle.

Holmes thought a moment, then nodded his head to the south. "We'll take the Laramie way. And if we don't find Marjory in that direction, we'll come back and follow the Platte. Then we'll show up at that rendezvous in June if we've still had no luck. And if no one can help us there, we'll ride to Santa Fe. I won't stop looking until I find her, or die in the search."

Cross was sorry he had asked. He was absolutely loyal to the Colonel, and they had been friends too long for Cross to even consider abandoning him now. Both he and Hampstead would follow Holmes into perdition's flames and back, if it meant bringing Marjory home safely to Missouri . . . and that was exactly what it was beginning to look like they might have to do.

Chapter Five

Bull Jackson gave his horse a moment to blow, then tugged the cinch belts tighter. As he worked, he became aware of the light hand he was using on the animal, and with sudden anger he grabbed the cinch and gave it a sharp pull, roughly working the buckles with his thick fingers.

You be careful around my kitchen, William, he heard his mother admonish, and the words that came back to him over the years rang as loudly and as clearly as if Lucy Jackson had been standing right behind him. A shudder ran up his huge frame. His mother had gone to Glory more than five years earlier. He knew it was crazy, but just the same, Bull Jackson glanced over his shoulder.

All he saw was all that he really expected to see. His partner, Kit Carson, straddling a fallen tree trunk and working the blade of his tomahawk on a sharpening stone.

Again an uncontrollable anger rose within him as

more memories came back. Why it should still happen, he didn't understand. All of that had taken place so many years before.

William! Gracious, you tromp through here like a wild bull! Go on out and play with the other boys now, and do be careful you don't hurt anyone. Mrs. Helgenbaugh came by yesterday and told me you nearly wrenched poor little Fritz's arm when you two was playing.

Bull growled out his anger, giving the bedroll behind his saddle a sharp shake to test the straps that held it in place. He couldn't help it if Fritz Helgenbaugh had been a sissy and a mamma's boy. He couldn't help it that he had towered over all the other boys his age, or that his strength at thirteen had been equal to that of a full-grown man.

William, dear, why do you spend all day long with a nose buried in a book? Go on out and play with the other boys.

He wanted to say, *Because they make fun of me, mamma, and then I get mad, and when I get mad, someone gets hurt. I can't help it. God, why did you make me so different?*

Then another voice: *William, come sit here on the porch swing with me. Would you like to kiss me?*

Sarah? Bull shook his head, but the voice would not go away. He was suddenly sweating in the chill morning air. He desperately wanted to forget, for he knew what must follow.

Come, William. You have such strong arms. I feel so safe when you are near me. Put your arm over my shoulder. It's all right. Robert is not here now, and he won't ever know anyway. Now, kiss me . . .

"No!"

Over on the tree trunk where he had been sitting, waiting for Ozzie Warner to return, Kit Carson looked up at his friend. "You say something to me, Bull?"

Bull grinned sheepishly, feeling suddenly foolish. "I

was talking to my horse. The blame fool animal nearly put a hoof down on my foot."

Kit grinned and went back to sharpening his tomahawk while Bull tried desperately to shake off that haunting episode in his past which had so often come, uninvited, to the doorway of his memory.

From the trees behind the cabin came a rifle shot. The sound of it brought Kit to his feet, and for Bull, it instantly slammed shut that unwanted portal to the past.

"That came from . . ."

"Ozzie!" Kit said, finishing Bull's sentence for him.

Another rifle shot rang out, and a second later the more subdued report of a pistol. Kit thrust his tomahawk under his belt and snatched up the rifle from where it leaned against a tree, with Bull right at his heels.

They plunged into the forest behind the cabin, and taking a steep slope in full stride, reached the top with their lungs burning. Kit hardly paused, but Bull, having to lug around so much more weight, drew to a stop and spent a quarter of a minute trying to catch his breath. Then he forged on after the nimble figure of Kit Carson a few hundred feet ahead.

What seemed to Kit an interminable run ended abruptly at a clearing, and as he broke free of the trees and wheeled to a stop, he saw Ozzie Warner laying face down, his head cleaved wide open, blood and brains spilled out upon the bright spring grass. Kit made a quick turn around the clearing, rifle at ready, but other than Billy Wilson standing stone-rigid with his back against a tree, his face drained of all color, and his blue eyes wide and staring, filled with horror, there was no one else around.

"What happened?" Kit demanded, but the boy was too terrified to speak.

At that moment Bull came crashing through the undergrowth. "Oh my God!" he groaned, staring at Ozzie.

Kit knelt beside Ozzie and saw that the trapper's rifle had been fired. There were tracks nearby, leading across the clearing into the trees to the north. Kit looked back at Billy. The boy was still white with fear.

"There were three shots," Kit said, and at that moment he heard movement in the trees where the track led off and he swung his rifle.

Seth Wilson burst into view, a rifle in one hand, a pistol in the other. "I think I winged one of them!" Wilson said, his voice edged with excitement. In the next moment, the older man, Sam, appeared from another direction, and he looked as if he had been doing some heavy running too.

"There was two or three of 'em," Sam said, breathing hard.

Kit lowered his rifle as Seth came forward. "Who did this?" he demanded.

"I only caught a glimpse of them, but they looked like Utes. Lucky your friend managed to get off a shot and that me and Sam was nearby, or they would have murdered my boy too." Seth Wilson went to the lad and put an arm over his shoulder. "I'm going to take him back to the cabin. He's seen enough here." Wilson started away.

"Hold up there," Kit barked, narrowing an eye at the trapper. "Your boy is the only witness we have to what happened. I intend to ask him some questions."

"Later. Can't you see he's white as a sheet? And he ain't been well. Ain't that right, Billy? Tell the man."

To Kit's left, Sam Wilson slowly leveled his rifle in a casual way, not intending it to be noticed. At the same time Seth's grip tightened upon the boy's neck until the lad winced and gritted his teeth.

Softly Billy said, "I . . . I didn't see anything. It all happened too fast, mister."

"There, he told you. Now I'm taking him back to the cabin. I warned you boys about the Indian trouble we've been having. You didn't listen and now one of you is dead. Take your friend there and bury him. Then ride out of here. If you ain't gone by noon, I'll send you on your way with a bullet."

Seth turned Billy around, shoving the boy roughly ahead. Sam remained in the clearing, a tight grin upon his gaunt face, his rifle still casually pointing in Kit and Bull's direction.

"You boys better pull out now like my brother says. Do what you have to for your friend, then saddle up and ride."

Although Sam made it sound casual, Kit knew they were being run out at gunpoint. Anger rose like foul bile in his throat, and his fist squeezed the rifle in his hand. With the eye of a hunter and the cunning of an Indian fighter, Kit measured Sam Wilson and knew he could take him if he wanted to. But there had already been one man killed, and although Kit despised bad manners, manners alone wasn't a serious enough crime in his book to warrant another killing.

Kit turned his back to Sam and said to Bull, "Let's bury him proper. I don't know if he had kin back east, do you?"

"Other than his pa somewhere, I don't recollect him talking about any other kin." Bull handed Kit his rifle, then lifted Ozzie light as a feather into his arms.

In spite of Bull's size and strength, there was a gentleness there that Kit noted just then. As if Bull was fully aware of the power in his arms, and he was making a conscious effort to control it, as if someone in the past had admonished him for its misuse. Bull carried the body of their fallen friend back to their camp, and finding a shovel in the lean-to barn, he dug a hole, flinging the dirt tirelessly until it was deep enough. They laid Ozzie in it, covered it over, and Bull read a verse out of the Psalms from his Bible. All the while, Seth watched them out the window of the cabin.

"There isn't anything else left here to do, Kit," Bull said, glancing back. "That man watching us from the corner of his window makes my neck-hairs tingle. Let's ride."

"Not yet, Bull. I've got a thing or two I want to check out."

"You heard him. We leave by noon, or he begins to unload lead in our direction."

Kit glanced at the angle of the sun, a faint grin making its way past the somber look that had been there through the humble funeral service. "Well, the way I read it, we still got some time left." He shoved a pistol into his belt and grabbed up the rifle. "I want to give that clearing a better look before we pull out. We might find something important."

Bull followed Kit back to where Ozzie had been killed. Immediately the tracker instinct took over as Kit stooped to examine the impressions made in the grass. Slowly he followed the tracks to the edge of the clearing, his keen eyes looking for other signs. In the thick wood beyond the clearing Kit studied a patch of last year's pine needles that had been crushed down over an area of a couple of square feet. Frowning, he glanced up at an outcropping of rock where any trace would be difficult to follow, and spent a few minutes walking along the outcropping before returning to the spot Ozzie had fallen. Then he went off along the trail from which Sam had come upon the scene. Seth had apparently arrived first, and the Indians' tracks had been obscured by Seth's chase. For all that had happened here, the scene of Ozzie's murder was woefully thin on footprints.

"Well?"

Kit frowned, his blue eyes narrowing. "It's mighty peculiar, Bull. It's unfortunate that Seth's footprints trampled out them of the Indians who did this, but even so, they must have been mighty light-footed. I tried to pick up the trail beyond where he chased them down, but them Utes was smart. They took to hard ground right off. It might be hours before I cipher their trail. By then they'll have had time to rejoin their party."

"What are we gonna do?"

"There's still the girl. If we find the band that took her, we might discover who murdered Ozzie too." He shook his head. "It's mighty peculiar," he repeated. "The Utes have always been of a friendly persuasion. I don't understand what changed 'em."

Bull nudged him with an elbow and inclined his head toward the top of the hill. "He's keeping us in his sights, Kit."

Kit glanced over, then dismissed Seth Wilson, who had appeared on the hill above the clearing with a rifle in the crook of his arm. "Still ain't noon yet, Bull. Let him exercise his eyeballs all he wants to."

Kit poked around the clearing a few minutes more, then they returned to their horses, and loaded Ozzie's gear onto his animal. They swung up onto their saddles and rode away as Seth Wilson watched from behind his window.

"Can't say as I'm sorry to say good-bye to that place," Bull commented when the trees closed in behind them.

Kit remained grimly silent as he set his course to the west, keeping Laramie Peak to his right. He'd left a friend behind, and that made him both angry and heavy-hearted, but that the men responsible for his death might go unpunished rankled most of all. If there was one thing Kit had learned early on while growing up on the edge of civilization in Missouri, and then later when he had come west, it was that you never let violent men go unpunished. Only swift retribution would keep the peace in a land where violence is so easily perpetrated, and too rarely punished.

He picked up a trail that snaked up over the Laramie Range. Several hours later they reined to a stop on a high ridge where the two trappers had a sweeping view of the vast Laramie Plains far below, all the way to the Snowy Mountains on the other side, some thirty or forty miles to the west. It was wide, wild country; home not only to the Utes, but the Arapaho, Crow, and Cheyenne. Far to the north he watched an immense herd of buffalo drift like vast shadow across this sea of grass.

"I can see it in your face, Kit. You've been pondering mighty hard on something ever since we left Wilson's place this morning. You haven't said but five words all day, and three of those were grunts."

Kit's eyes remained fixed on the distant Laramie Plains, a part of his brain thinking that tomorrow they would be crossing it, and planning the best way to do that without arousing the curiosity of any passing Crow or Arapaho hunting party. But the other part had heard Bull's thinly veiled question.

"You know, Bull, if I step on a rattlesnake, I just naturally expect it to come around and strike at me. If I jab a mad dog with a stick, I expect it to bite. If I pet a cat, well I expect it will—"

"Purr," Bull finished, catching Kit's drift. "But what has that got to do with anything?"

"Well, I reckon what I'm saying is this. You come to expect a particular behavior from a thing; a rattlesnake, a dog, a cat . . . or a Ute."

Bull nodded his big, hairy head, suddenly understanding. "In other words, you are wondering what has happened to make the Utes, or at least one band of the Utes, start acting differently than they have been?"

Kit considered a moment. "Could it be men like Seth and his brother who changed them?"

An odd glimmer entered Bull's eyes. "Sometimes men just change," he said in a tone that made Kit think that somehow Bull had a deeper knowledge of such things than he wanted to let on.

Bull winced behind his thick, black beard. "I once knew a fellow back in Virginia who had a temper like old Pharaoh had locusts. He'd bust your head if you looked at him crosswise. And when it came to drinking, there wasn't a bar in Fairfax County safe from wreck and ruin. He spent many a night in the county jail because he busted up some bartender or cracked a few noggins. And he was big enough to do a right proper job of it too."

"What came of this friend of yours, Bull?"

"Ruin, sad to say. He came to ruin, and it wasn't at the hands of the law, or a vigilance committee of angry citizens, raising up arms against him. It came from the most unlikeliest place you can imagine."

"I can imagine some mighty unlikely ways a man can come to ruin." Kit grinned, although he felt that right then Bull was talking from his heart, and not just of some curious incident that happened long ago.

Bull grimaced, a far-off sadness suddenly in his eyes. "It came from the sweetest, gentlest creature God ever put on this green earth, Kit. It came at the hands of a woman. And the strangest thing was, she really cared for him. Deep down in her heart, she really *cared* for him!" Bull fell into a long silence.

"What happened, Bull?" Kit asked quietly.

"She had a great affection for this fellow, but unfortunately there was another man in her life too. You see, she was a married woman—married to a heavy-handed, evil-mouthed tyrant who kept her locked away in a big house in the middle of a thousand acres of tobacco, surrounded by twenty slaves. He never allowed her to go off on her own. She was a virtual prisoner in her own home." The sudden anger that welled up in Bull's voice momentarily choked off his words.

"Like Billy Wilson?"

Bull glanced at his friend. "Yeah," he said with fervor. "Just like that poor kid."

This friend of yours, and the lady's husband, they come to fighting over the lady?"

Bull's eyes fixed upon the tawny sweep of the Laramie Plains. "My friend, he has a mighty fearful temper, and if he ain't as watchful as a man alone in Injun country, it can sneak right up on him. The two of them, they got to meeting in secret while the husband was away. Except one day he came back sooner than either of them had suspected. He caught them both in . . . well, let's just say she being a married woman, my friend ought to have known better. Her husband had his rights, and they had been trampled on. It came to blows, and when it was all over, the fellow was dead and my friend was suddenly a wanted man, on the run. Afterwards, my friend changed. He knew it was both his temper and poor judgment that had gotten him in such a fix, and from that day on, he swore he'd not hurt another man except to protect his own life, or someone else's. And you know what?"

"What?"

"He never let his temper get the better of him since, and he never done anything as thick-headed as getting cozy with another man's wife, either."

There was more to the story than Bull was telling, but Kit didn't press the matter. He said instead, "Because your friend changed, you suspect the Ute could change too?"

"Why not?"

Kit glanced out across the wide countryside. That the Utes had somehow turned hostile toward the white trappers was a possibility, but one that he was not yet prepared to accept—at least not without better proof than the words of Seth Wilson. It might have been Arapaho, or Cheyenne, or. . . . The pieces didn't fit together, and Kit did not like unanswered questions.

Chapter Six

They reached the low-lying foothills by nightfall, and with the towering peaks of the Laramie Range now rising behind them, and the darkening plains ahead, Kit and Bull made camp in a copse of ash and cottonwood trees by a fast stream. Kit shot a deer and the two men ate well that night. Afterwards, they sat around the fire discussing tomorrow's ride.

"It's going to be a hard push," Kit said, pulling a burning twig from the fire and putting it to the bowl of his clay pipe. "I figure we need to make it across these plains and into the Snowy Range before sunset, and it would please me no end if we manage it without drawing unnecessary attention to ourselves."

"The Plains Indians are dangerous folk," Bull allowed, settling his bulk comfortably against a rock and stretching his long legs out, warming the soles of his moccasins near the small fire.

Kit knew this to be true, just as certainly as he knew that the Utes were tolerant of white travelers . . . or at least they had been the last time he'd met a band of them. That had been more than a year earlier when he had spent a couple of days camped with a band of Utes led by a friendly chief named Walkara. Walkara, or Walker as the whites called him, had treated him well. The Chief's only vice, it appeared to Kit at the time, had been his affection for fine horses, which he boasted he obtained from raids on California rancheros. Walkara was a tall, handsome fellow with broad shoulders and a hawkish nose. He spoke several Indian languages, a smattering of English, and was fluent in Spanish. Walkara liked fine clothing, silver encrusted bridles, and wives . . . lots of wives!

Kit had been impressed by the Utes back then. Now, he wasn't so sure. He thought back on what Bull had said about folks changing, and started to ask Bull what had ever happened to his friend, but decided not to pry. The way Bull had spoken of it had given Kit an unsettled feeling, and he wasn't sure he wanted to know. If it was important, Bull would tell him sooner or later. If not, then it was none of his business anyway. Kit was not one to pry into another's affairs, nor did he take much pleasure in spreading loose gossip, or the "small talk" that some men brought to the campfire. Most of it, as far as Kit was concerned, amounted to no more than an excuse for men to brag on themselves.

They let their horses graze a while, then staked them out nearby. Dousing the fire to keep its glow from attracting attention to themselves, Kit and Bull crawled into their blankets, each taking his rifle to bed with him, just in case. As he lay there, staring up at the starry sky, his breath making gray puffs in the chill air, Kit wondered what Marjory Holmes was doing at this very moment. Was she even still alive? And if so, had she given up hope of rescue?

In a few minutes, Bull's rasping, throat-clearing snorts stopped and in their place came light, even breathing. Kit reminded himself of the heavy riding ahead of them come morning, and clearing the thoughts from his brain, he closed his eyes.

As sleep approached, a face floated briefly against his closed eyelids. It was a lovely face, framed in golden hair with bright blue, sad, frightened eyes. The vision startled him: so real, yet so impossible! As far as Kit could remember, he had never met the owner of the face before.

Then he was asleep.

On the other side of the Laramie Range, Gilbert McCaine had called a halt to their march. The men set up camp, built a mighty fire, and ate a hardy dinner. They were sitting around the flames, swapping tall tales, and making big plans for how they would spend the money they would get from the sale of their packs of beaver pelts when all at once someone called to them from out of the darkness.

"Hello, you men in camp!"

The sudden hail from the night instantly silenced the men sitting around the fire as hands reached for guns and knives.

"Who is it?" McCaine called back, easing out the pistol in his belt.

"Friends."

"If you're friends, then you have nothing to fear from us. Come on into the light."

In a moment three men stepped into view, leading their horses. They each carried a rifle in the crook of one arm, careful not to present a threatening bearing to the armed trappers of the camp. One of the men, apparently the leader, came forward a few steps.

"We saw your fire from a ways back. At first we thought you might be Indian. I'm mighty pleased to find that you're not."

"We're trappers," McCaine said, lowering his pistol in a gesture of friendship. "Recently out of winter quarters on the Green River. Bound for Fort William. My name is Gilbert McCaine. I'm the Booshway of this here party."

"We've just come from Fort William ourselves, Mr. Gilbert. I'm Colonel Willard Holmes, and these two men are my companions, Caleb Cross and Chester Hampstead."

The men shook hands. McCaine said, "Holmes, is it?"

"Yes." The colonel must have seen the concern that came to McCaine's face. "What is it?"

"You wouldn't happen to have a female kin would you, a girl by the name of Marjory?"

"Marjory!" The name fairly burst from Holmes's lips. "You know where she is?"

"Well, not exactly where, but we do know who she's with."

McCaine went on to tell Holmes the story just as he had heard it from Seth Wilson. When he finished, Holmes described the events that had led up to his daughter's kidnapping, and the heartbreaking pursuit that had followed.

"Captain Sublette said that I might get word of my daughter from you Rocky Mountain boys. This is the first bit of encouragement we've had since leaving Independence."

"Well, here's another bit of news you might find hopeful. We was traveling with three other men when we learned of your daughter's fate. They stayed behind to have a look for her. One of them is a fellow by the name of Kit Carson who's about the best tracker I've ever met."

It was wonderful news. Colonel Holmes unsheathed the portrait of Marjory and showed it around. The men all agreed that Marjory was about as pretty as a spring columbine; as pleasing to look upon as the pearly gates might be to a confirmed sinner an instant after drawing his last breath. But since not a one of the trappers had lain eyes on a white woman for nearly a year, a sack of potatoes gussied up in female finery might have gotten their pulses to quicken too.

Afterwards, McCaine sketched a map of the mountain ranges in their vicinity for the searchers. Some of the trappers lent a hand, and in the end Holmes had a clear idea of what lay before him, and where he might expect to find Ute Indians camped. Thus armed with this information, Holmes, Cross, and Hampstead made plans for the next day's march.

Soon, very soon now, Holmes thought later, lying beneath his blanket, trying to sleep but unable to. He felt he was closing in, his only regret was that the four trappers who had committed this offense had not lived to suffer at his hands. Just the same, the Utes who now held his daughter would pay dearly for their part in Marjory's sufferings.

In the crisp chill of predawn, Kit and Bull saddled their horses beneath a gray sky where the burnished underbellies of clouds were just beginning to glow orange. Neither man spoke much. They had the long ride before them on their minds, and each felt the uneasiness that came with knowing ahead lay thirty miles of danger before the relative safety of mountains once again closed around them.

A couple of hours later, the sun had cleared the high peaks of the Laramie Range and shown full upon the two riders striding out across the wide grass plains. Kit had put his horse into an easy lope that easily ate up the miles, but not their horses' reserves. He kept up a constant vigil as they rode. The sun climbed higher and now it burned hot upon the backs of both men. If they stopped to rest, it might mean riding at night, or spending that night in a cold camp out on these plains, for a campfire would be seen for miles in every direction.

Kit judged it to be about noon when they came to the crest of a hill and reined up. To the west loomed the Snowy Range, much closer now; behind them the Laramie Range had receded. There was a dark range of mountains lying to the south, just off the horizon, and when he looked to the north, the grass seemed to stretch on forever. The North Platte River was somewhere off in that direction, many, many miles away.

Bull swung off his animal, sleeved sweat from his brow, and wiped it from the band of his hat. "I'd judge we're about halfway across, Kit."

"We've made pretty good time, Bull." Kit stepped out of the saddle too and the men led their mounts down the slope to a rill running along a sandy wash. Horses and men drank deeply and then lingered in the shade of a lone cottonwood tree a few minutes before pushing on again.

An hour later the Snowy Range seemed much closer, and Kit was beginning to breathe easier. All at once a movement far to the south caught his eye. He drew rein and stood absolutely still; on open ground a moving object was easier to spot than a motionless one.

"They look like Cheyenne," Bull said. "Wonder why they're in such a hurry?"

"Could be Arapaho," Kit commented, straining to see the line of mounted warriors a mile or so off. They were riding hard, their horses stretching out, the warriors bent low along the animals' backs. "Let me have your spyglass."

Bull reached back into his saddlebags and handed Kit the glass. Kit extended it and put it to his eye. The riders now appeared much closer in the circular field of view. Kit saw the war lances in their hands, the bows slung across their shoulders, and their hair streaming back in the wind of their pounding flight.

"Cheyenne," he informed Bull as he moved the glass along the column. "Seven, eight . . . twelve, fourteen . . . Thar's sixteen of 'em."

"What's put them in such an all-fire hurry, I wonder?"

Kit put the glass on the lead warrior, then moved it ahead and there he had it! No more that a quarter mile in front of the Cheyenne was another horse, racing across the plains as if the devil himself was on its tail. Upon the fleeing animal was a man dressed in a long, black coat and wearing a black hat which he had plastered to his head with his left hand while his right hand slapped the reins madly, and his heels flailed the horse's flanks without mercy.

"Thar's the reason," Kit exclaimed, passing the spyglass back to Bull.

"What are we gonna do about it?" Bull asked a moment later when he had lowered the glass.

"I don't see that we have any choice," Kit said, driving his heels into his horse's flanks and taking off at an angle that would cut across that of the man in the black coat and his pursuers. They pounded down a slope, then up the side of a low, rolling hill. Cresting it, Kit urged his horse on to greater speed, crossing into their line of sight and flagging his rifle over his head to draw their attention.

The man saw the signal and immediately turned his horse toward Kit and Bull. The Cheyenne saw it too. They were close enough to unleash a volley of arrows that arched at the fleeing man and whizzed past him like angry hornets, hitting the ground on either side and in front of the horse.

Kit released Ozzie's horse and the animal galloped along beside him as his own horse flew at the Indians. Taking the reins in his mouth, Kit shouldered his rifle and fired. No more than two hundred yards separated them now, and his bullet struck one of the warriors, knocking him off his horse. The Cheyenne moved apart, making them harder to hit. Bull's rifle boomed, but his bullet missed.

Then the fleeing man was among them, and after turning their horses, they rode like the wind, trying to outdistance the Indians. But it was soon apparent that outrunning them was not going to be possible. An arrow whizzed past Kit's ear, another made a long arc overhead and thunked into the ground in front of him. Kit fired a pistol over his shoulder as he hurriedly scanned the wide country for cover. But there wasn't a single tree for the three of them to squeeze behind.

Then he spied what he thought at first was a buffalo wallow ahead. Driving his horse on, he angled towards it. The animal sprang over the edge of it, and Kit realized it was deeper that any buffalo-made wallow he'd ever seen. They had chanced upon a natural watering hole. Kit reined in hard and his horse's tail brushed the ground as its hind legs dug in. He sprang out of the saddle even as Bull and the stranger were attempting to pull their horses to a stop. Clambering up the side of the wide depression and stretching out on his belly, Kit quickly reloaded his rifle, and sighting on the nearest rider, touched the trigger. A cloud of gray gunsmoke bloomed in front of him. Fifty yards away, another Cheyenne burrowed into the ground.

Then Bull and the stranger were beside him, their rifles booming, and for the next few minutes they kept up a steady, ear-ringing barrage. Two more Cheyenne were punched off the backs of their horses before the Indians finally moved off, out of rifle range, and circled up to make new plans.

Kit reloaded and looked at Bull. "That was a close one."

"Too close for my liking!" Bull whipped off his hat and patted his forehead with a red handkerchief. "And we still aren't out of the frying pan."

"That's an understatement if I've ever heard one," the stranger said, running a ball down the barrel of his rifle. His back was towards them, and that tall, black beaver hat bobbed up and down as he spoke while finishing the reloading. Capping his rifle, he peered over the edge of the wallow at the powwow taking place just beyond their range. "That old blackguard, Yellow Wolf, never was what one might call hospitable."

"They'll be back," Kit assured them. "Just as soon as

they figure out how to do so without eating any more of our lead." Kit squinted at the warriors in the distance. The man in charge was a tough, wiry little man who appeared to be in his forties and looked as if he ate horseshoe nails for breakfast. "You say that's Yellow Wolf? Ain't Yellow Wolf a chief of the Cheyenne dog soldiers?"

"He is, indeed," the stranger said.

"Why was he after you?"

"Oh, Yellow Wolf has hated me ever since I was a kid and stole two of his prized horses."

"You?" Kit looked at the man who at that moment turned from his position on the rim of the hollow and smiled back at him.

Bull gasped, and Kit's mouth dropped. The man doffed his hat, grinning, as two long braids of black hair tumbled out of it.

"You're an Injun!" Kit blurted.

"An Injun!" Bull roared, as if an echo to Kit's own amazement.

The man shrugged his shoulders. "Waldo Gray Feather Smith, at your service, sir. And yes, I confess to the sins of my mother."

Kit cranked his mouth shut.

Bull rolled his eyes, then looked heavenward and muttered, "O let me not be mad, not mad sweet heaven! Keep me in temper."

The Indian glanced at Bull, his grin widening. "King Lear, act one, scene five."

Chapter Seven

"Ute?"

"Well, half of me is Ute. The wise half, according to my mother, but then she's Ute herself."

"Oh, yeah?" Bull growled. "Then what's the dumb half?"

"English."

"English! Why, if that ain't the most arrogant—" Bull cut himself off in mid sentence, then went on, "and where in the devil did you ever learn Shakespeare?"

They were sitting at the bottom of the wallow, near a small pool of clear water. Kit was up on the rim, keeping an eye on the Cheyenne, who had begun to slowly ride a wide circle around their position, as if trying to discover some means to penetrate it.

Waldo brushed at the muddy stains on his tall hat. "Harvard. Class of '32. I studied English drama . . . at my father's insistence."

"Why was that? To smarten up the dumber half?"

Waldo grinned.

"And what the devil are you doing out here, anyway? Why aren't you back east with your Harvard schoolmates, drinking tea and eating English crumpets?"

"What am *I* doing here?" Waldo said, amazed. "I was born here, Mr. Jackson. I might ask you the same question."

"Will you two quit fighting," Kit said, looking over his shoulder at them. "Save it for the Cheyenne."

Bull snorted. "We nearly got ourselves killed rescuing an Injun from a pack of Injuns. It don't hardly make sense, Kit."

"And I can't thank you enough for that," Waldo gushed, tugging his hat back onto his head and taking his rifle up the side of the watering hole to where Kit was keeping an eye on Yellow Wolf and his warriors. They watched the circling Cheyenne a while, then Waldo said, "You would think that after all these years Yellow Wolf would get over the loss of a few mangy horses."

"Mangy? You said they was his prize horses," Kit reminded him.

Waldo gave a short laugh. "What do Cheyenne know about horses? To Yellow Wolf they were just dandy. But to a Ute?" Waldo made a face. "They were good for nothing more than eating. In fact, that's just what we did with them."

"How did they get onto you, Waldo?"

"It was the most innocent thing, Mr. Carson."

"Call me Kit. Everyone else does."

"Very well, Kit. Well, I was passing near their camp and a couple warriors rode out to investigate. Seems they mistook me for a white man, and were contemplating taking my scalp for their lodge pole."

Waldo looked down at himself and plucked at the sleeve of his black coat. "I ought to discard these duds for something more appropriate now that I'm back out west," he said, distracted.

Doug Hawkins

"What happened when they discovered you were Ute?"

"They weren't sure what to do with me then. I was a curiosity at first, then a dilemma. Apparently the Cheyenne and Ute aren't at war with each other—at least, not this year. They had about decided to let me go on my way when one of the men recognized me. The next thing I knew they were hauling me back to their camp circle, bragging about how Yellow Wolf was going to be pleased now that he would finally get his hands on me. That sounded rather ominous, if you catch my meaning, Kit, so I managed to break rank and light out of there. I had a good head start too, and I could have lost them if my horse had been of a better character."

Kit grinned. "Was it a Cheyenne horse?"

Waldo shook his head, a frown drawing down the corners of his mouth. "No, it's even worse than that. It's an eastern-bred saddle horse."

Bull crawled up besides them at that moment. "Ain't he the most insolent redskin you ever did meet, Kit? I say we throw him back to Yellow Wolf. It might keep them Cheyenne off our hind ends long enough to ske-daddle out of here. After all, it's his people's fault that were in this fix in the first place."

"My people? How did we Utah Indians get you in this fix? If you must place blame anywhere, put it where it belongs; on me."

Kit explained it to Waldo, and when he finished, Waldo huffed indignantly and said, "That's ridiculous! My people do not take white women captive! Horses, yes. Cattle, sometimes. White women, never! I shall accompany you Chief Walkara's village to prove it."

"That is, if we can get ourselves out of this tight spot," Kit noted wryly.

They watched the Cheyenne come together a safe distance away and discuss the matter. The sun stood overhead, turning the wallow into an oven. Bull crawled down to the bottom and tasted the water, declaring it

70

drinkable—but only just barely. An hour passed, then two.

"They're just sitting out there, waiting!" Bull complained, sighting along the barrel of his rifle. He set it back down. "If only them red bastards would drift a couple hundred feet my way," he said wistfully.

"Lucky they have no guns," Waldo noted, optimistically.

"They don't need guns. All they have to do is sit there and wait until we run out of food, or until the sun fries our brains." Kit shielded his eyes from the glare of the clear blue sky above.

"Food. You did have to bring that up," Bull groused. "Still got some of last night's venison in my saddlebags."

"Maybe they'll just go away," Waldo said with what Kit thought was a hopeful tone.

"And maybe Monday will come after Tuesday."

Waldo glanced over at Kit. "What do you suggest?"

Kit didn't have an answer to that . . . yet. But he was working on a scheme even then.

Colonel Holmes and his companions made good time crossing the Laramie Range by following the river all the way. They emerged on the western slope about twenty miles south of the point Kit and Bull had begun their crossing. At this point the plains narrowed as they swept south, and the Snowy Range was only twenty miles distant. As night stretched across the open land, Holmes dismounted and arched his tired back, kneading it as he started for a large outcropping. The men had ridden hard since leaving the trappers' camp that morning, and now everyone was ready to rest. But as Holmes stood upon a promontory of rock watching the sun sink behind the Snowy Range, both Caleb and Chester glanced at each other, suspecting that a pleasant campfire and cup of hot coffee was only a far-off dream.

"We'll push on," Holmes said, climbing down from the rock. "Another four or five hours will get us across these plains and into those mountains."

"In the dark?" Chester Hampstead asked, his reluctance showing.

"In the dark," Holmes affirmed sharply, then he glanced at the two men who had ridden with him these many months, and paused to remind himself that this was no longer Old Hickory's war, and he was no longer their commanding officer. That part of their lives had ceased almost twenty years ago. He had been driving them so hard that he'd nearly forgotten that these men had families back in Missouri, and farms, and friends, and all of that had suffered on his account. He added gently, "You men are tired—we're all tired. Perhaps I haven't told you how much I appreciate you sticking with me all these months."

"Shoot, Colonel, you're our friend," Caleb said. "Besides, I've known Meg since the day she was born. I couldn't look myself in the mirror if I pulled out of this here hunt knowing she was still out there somewhere, in the hands of them villains. Chester, he feels the same, don't you?"

Hampstead nodded his head. "You wanting to push on is understandable, Colonel, this being the first lead we've gotten after all these months. Caleb and me, we're with you all the way."

Holmes smiled at the two of them. "A man couldn't ask for better friends." He glanced at the darkening sky. "A half hour from now it won't make any difference if it's nine or three. It will be just as dark. Maybe we ought to make some coffee and eat something now, while we can. We'll rest here an hour or two, then push on. If we can make it across these plains tonight, we won't have to worry about the Cheyenne or Arapaho like McCaine warned us."

"I'll get a fire started," Chester volunteered, and went to gather up some wood.

The Colonel's Daughter

Caleb and Holmes began to loosen the cinches on their saddles. All at once Caleb pointed at something out on the Laramie Plains. "What's that, Colonel?"

Holmes squinted, then said, "It looks like a horse, and it seems to be coming this way."

A few minutes later the animal had stopped a few hundred yards out and was just standing there, watching them. Caleb quickly retightened the cinches and swung up onto his saddle. The runaway horse shied as he approached, but after one or two attempts, it allowed Caleb to grab the dangling reins and lead it back to their fire. The men gathered around and Holmes yanked an arrow from the bedroll tied behind the saddle.

"Now we know how it came to be running free," he said gloomily, "and that McCaine wasn't exaggerating about the dangers."

"I feel sorry for the rider," Chester said.

"Any blood on the saddle?" Caleb asked, but it was getting too dark to see, even if there had been.

"Wonder who the poor fellow was," Chester said.

"Maybe there's something here that will tell us." Holmes removed the saddle and carried it to the fire. Looking through the personal effects, they discovered a book with the name scribbled on the flyleaf.

"Ozzie Warner?" Holmes frowned. "McCaine said there were three men who set off to rescue Marjory: Carson, Jackson . . . and Warner."

A cloud of despair settled around the men. Caleb said, "Suppose it's the same fellow?"

"I don't see how it can be any other." Holmes stood abruptly and stared off into the night. "So, their attempt to rescue Marjory has failed, and three men have died."

"We can't know that for certain, Colonel," Hampstead allowed.

"No, but we can assume so. And we can assume that, without further evidence, it was the Utes who did this."

Caleb's long, hollow-cheeked face turned down to the

73

arrow in his hand. "Wish I could read these signs painted on this shaft. It would tell us for certain who did this."

"If they were any eastern tribe, I might be able to," Holmes said, "but none of us is familiar with these western tribes."

"I'll bet that Captain Sublette would know."

"Perhaps," Holmes said somberly. "Unfortunately, Captain Sublette is not here. We must assume the worst; that the same people who have my Marjory are the very savages who murdered those three trappers."

"I'll get that coffee going, Colonel, then we can be on our way," Chester Hampstead said with renewed urgency in his voice.

Twenty miles to the north, Kit was putting on a pot of coffee too. He had made a fire with the buffalo chips that littered the ground about the watering hole. The small pool of water at the bottom of it had proved to be a blessing which the men soon learned to appreciate as the day had grown long and hot. All the while, the Cheyenne remained just out of reach of their rifles, and as the land darkened, three campfires sprouted on the prairie, each at a different location around the wallow.

"They're making good and certain we don't try and skedaddle outta here tonight, Kit," Bull observed wryly when he'd come off the rim and hunkered down by the fire. "Reckon we might get a chance to sneak off once those Cheyenne settle down for the night?"

Kit glanced at the wedge of moon climbing amongst the stars. "Unless we all suddenly became ghosts, Bull, something I sincerely hope doesn't happen anytime soon, I don't see how. They won't sleep tonight, and if we want to keep our hair, neither will we."

"You expecting an attack?"

"It's what I would do if I was in their moccasins."

Waldo was on lookout at the rim of the hollow, listening to Kit and Bull's words. "We might crawl our way our of here, if we make believe we're snakes."

"Maybe," Kit replied, "but I ain't yet been able to teach that worthless old eastern-bred plug how to crawl on its belly. Maybe you Utes got a trick or two up your sleeves about horses you can teach me?"

Waldo gave a short laugh. "I wasn't planning to take the horses, Kit."

Kit put a twist of flaming grass to his pipe and got his tobacco glowing in the clay bowl. "Then I don't reckon you were planning to make it very far, were you?"

The coffee was done, and Kit took a cup of it. Afterwards, he crawled up alongside the Ute and said, "I'll spell you a while, Waldo."

"You know, Kit, now that I'm back in the land of my people, maybe it would be smarter if I went by my Indian name, Gray Feather. That way I won't stand out any in the eyes of my mother's people."

Kit laughed. "Your name can't hold a candle to those fancy duds."

Waldo grinned. "I intend to rectify that matter as soon as we're out of this hole."

"*Rectify*? Now, that's another thing you need to work on, Gray Feather. No Injun I ever met uses such words. Shoot, I ain't even sure *I* know what it means." Kit scanned the darkness the lay beyond the soft glow from their little fire at the bottom of the watering hole, waiting for his eyes to fully adjust. "Go get yourself something to eat, Gray Feather. And there's coffee too, that is if Harvard-educated Indians drink the stuff."

Waldo grinned. "With alacrity!"

Kit scowled at him.

Waldo's grin faltered, drooping into a frown. He cleared his throat and said, "This Injun drink much black water! Mmmm, good."

"That's better, Gray Feather. Now you're beginning to sound like Injuns I know."

The moon drifted across the sky and constellations made their slow, nightly rotation. Kit, Bull, and Gray

Feather had stationed themselves around the rim of the watering hole, hugging their rifles, each peering off in a different direction. Kit had been pondering the problem of their escape almost from the very moment they had plunged frantically into this hole earlier that day. It was plain they couldn't outrun the Cheyenne, and they certainly couldn't outwait them—there were twelve of them, and Kit and his two companions couldn't hope to stay alert much longer without some sleep. Besides, although they had a source of water, their food was miserably low, and the blazing sun would make another day trapped in this giant reflector about the nearest thing to hell that Kit hoped he'd ever experience.

He felt a little like he did when the two grizzlies had run him up that tree. Only difference was, he knew the bears would get bored and wander off—eventually. He held no such hope for the Cheyenne doing the same.

Kit suspected the Cheyenne would attack tonight, only they hadn't so far. What were they waiting for? A thought occurred to him and he slipped back down into the depression and began unrolling his bedroll.

"What you doing there, Kit, planning to take a nap?"

"Sure am, Bull. And I think you ought to do the same."

"You gone loco, Kit?"

"I hope not, but in a little while we'll see." Kit crawled up over the edge of the water hole and came back a few minutes later clutching an armful of prairie grass. After three trips, he had collected enough to construct a reasonable enough shape of a man beneath his blanket. Then he checked that the halter leads of their horse were securely fastened to a couple of large boulders.

"Think you can do the same, Bull?" he asked, easing up to the rim besides his partner.

Bull gave Kit a sharp scowl. "I could, if I knew why I was doing it."

"A decoy?" Gray Feather inquired.

"Something like that."

Bull frowned, but didn't ask any more questions and slipped down to the bottom of the hollow. In ten minutes he had filled his blanket with grass and was back. "I had to collect a mite more grass than you, Kit," he complained.

Kit grinned and looked over at Gray Feather. "You said something about shucking them fancy duds?"

"Right now?"

"Unless you want to spend another day here, and meet Yellow Wolf face-to-face tomorrow, now would be a good time."

"I haven't got anything on underneath."

"Just the coat and hat will do."

Gray Feather crawled down below the rim so the Cheyenne wouldn't see what he was doing, and in the next few minutes managed to sneak over the edge and haul back enough grass to stuff the coat. Kit arranged it on the edge of the hollow in plain sight of the Cheyenne, and as a final gesture, he placed the tall hat prominently atop it.

"Just what have you got in mind?" Bull demanded when they had come together at the bottom.

"So long as there were three of us keeping watch, Yellow Wolf knew he'd never sneak in and take us by surprise. He could overpower us, of course, but why take a chance on losing men if just waiting us out would get him what he wanted? But if he thought that only a single guard was watching, he might risk sending a raiding party."

"Now that we fixed it up to look like we're asleep, where will the real us be?"

Kit pointed to the dummy up on the rim of the hollow. "Right in front of Gray Feather, maybe ten or fifteen feet out in the grass. If Yellow Wolf takes our bait, the only sensible thing to do is to sneak up on Gray Feather's blind side."

Gray Feather nodded his head. "You think like an Indian, Kit."

Kit said, "They'll slip down the back side of this here hollow, and if the horses don't give them away, they'll try to slit the throats of our grass friends. When they discover they've been fooled, that's when we open fire. If I haven't missed my guess, Yellow Wolf has let some of his men go to sleep. At most, we might have six or seven to contend with." Kit hefted his pistol and rifle. "I'll account for two of them, and so will you, Bull. Gray Feather's rifle will make it five. That should even up the odds some."

"It just might work," Bull allowed.

"Once we scatter them, we'll scramble for our horses and light a shuck for those mountains. If we're lucky, we can shake them in the dark."

"And if we're not, our horses will break a leg in a prairie dog hole and we'll break our necks," Gray Feather observed matter-of-factly.

Chapter Eight

Kit remained in the hollow until Bull first, and then Gray Feather, had had enough time to slip over the rim and snake their way into the grass that ringed the watering hole like the circle of hair on a bald man's head. After Kit had determined that his partners were nestled down and snug in the tall grass, he eased up and peered over. The three Indian camps were dark, and he wondered if maybe Yellow Wolf wasn't trying to play the same game as he was. It was tempting to sneak on over and find out exactly what was going on, but Kit reined in his natural curiosity. They had decided on a plan of action, and he would see it played out to the end.

He worked his way into his position—one of three they had all agreed upon—and settled down for what might be a long wait. It was deadly quiet out there on the black Laramie Plains in the middle of the night, and except for the occasional yap of a coyote keeping a safe distance from them, or the hoot of a prairie owl, it was as still as a graveyard. Kit would have liked to have had his blanket just then as the early morning chill settled in his bones, but the blanket was presently employed keeping the chill from a pile of grass.

He put the discomfort out of mind and concentrated on the rim of the hollow, and the unmoving shape of Gray Feather's coat and hat propped on it.

Hours passed.

Kit wondered how Bull and Gray Feather were managing the long wait. They had agreed not to try to communicate with each other, for there would be no way of knowing if at that very moment a stealthy Cheyenne might not be creeping past. Kit just had to trust they were still awake and watching the watering hole as he was.

How many more hours passed? Kit could only estimate. The moon had dropped behind the peaks of the Snowy range. It was the darkest period of the night, the hour or so before dawn. Kit was beginning to fear he had badly misread the Indians' intentions. . . .

Then something moved. Kit strained at the far edge of the hollow, seeing only by starlight now, waiting, hardly breathing. The form of a man appeared on the lighter-colored dirt of the hollow. Then another crawled up beside him. One by one Cheyenne appeared as if out of nowhere. They gathered around the rim, remaining for a while as motionless as the rocks of the moon. Then one of them moved, not down into the hollow as Kit suspected he might, but along its hard ridge, making his way slowly toward the stuffed coat and beaver hat.

In a moment that stalking Cheyenne would know the truth, and Kit and the others would have only a few seconds once he sounded the alarm. Kit quietly put the rifle to his shoulder and steadied its sights on the crouching man, but he dared not cock it yet. In this absolute silence, drawing back the heavy hammer would be like ringing an alarm bell.

The Indian hovered there a moment, crouched like a

cat about to pounce, then a knife appeared in his hand and he leaped . . .

Startled, the Indian stood, holding the black coat with its grass stuffing spilling out of it. At that moment, Kit drew back the hammer and touched the trigger.

The stillness was shattered by the boom and the flash of orange flame. Kit's bullet plowed the Indian off his feet, and almost before he had hit the ground two more shots exploded nearby. Kit leaped to his feet, brandishing his pistol and dashed onto the rim of the watering hole. An arrow zinged past his head. Kit drew a bead and parted the warrior's skull with his next shot.

He shoved the pistol under his belt, drew out his tomahawk, and hurled it at a Cheyenne nocking an arrow into his bowstring. The ax imbedded itself in the man's sternum. Another Cheyenne leaped for Kit, his knife gray in the starlight like a huge claw seeking Kit's heart. Kit dove under the Cheyenne's blade, hearing at that moment the report of a pistol. As he rolled back to his feet, he saw the Indian tumbling down the incline of the watering hole. Bull was a few paces off, lowering his pistol.

The rest of the attackers instantly disappeared in the night to regroup. "To the horses!" Kit shouted. He glanced around at the six unmoving forms scattered about, then yanked his tomahawk from the breast of the fallen Cheyenne and plunged into the hollow. Their skittish horses sidestepped and strained excitedly at their halter leads. Not wasting even an instant to untie the animals, the men slashed the ropes that held them to the boulders and leaped upon their saddles.

Even as their mounts scrambled up and out of the bowl of the watering hole, Kit saw that four riders were already riding hard from one of the Indian camps. He tugged his horse's head around the other way and dug his heals into its flanks, aiming for one of the gaps between the three camps.

In the blackness of the night the horses stretched out for all the speed they could summon, their hooves pounding the unseen ground, their manes flying back. The Indian camp swept past on Kit's left, and then they were in the open, racing across the tall grass valley, heedless of the dangers that the darkness held. Kit glanced over his shoulders in time to see Indians scrambling onto their animals to take up the pursuit. Bull and Gray Feather were both leaning low into the wind, whipping the ends of their reins across their mount's shoulders, flailing their flanks with their heels.

The clouds to the east, above the Laramie range, were beginning to show a faint tinge of pink. In another hour it would be light enough to see by, and Kit knew that if they could only maintain their lead until then, they'd have a clear shot at reaching the cover of the Snowy Range where he and his partners could make a proper stand against these savages.

But that was a mighty big and doubtful *if* right now.

Kit said a short prayer that their animals would not stumble or find a prairie dog hole. After that, there was nothing more that he could do than let the horse have its head and hold on for dear life.

Colonel Willard Holmes tapped the sole of Caleb Cross's foot with the toe of his boot. Caleb snorted and rolled beneath his blankets. "Time to get moving."

"What time is it, Colonel?" Cross mumbled, shaking off the sleep.

"Nearly dawn." Holmes crossed the campsite, hearing last year's pine needles crunching beneath his boots in the dark, and nudged the bulky form on the other side of their dead fire. "Chester, it's time."

As his two friends sat up and rubbed the sleep from their eyes, Holmes built up a small fire and prepared coffee. They'd been living on jerky and the wild game they could shoot along the way. This morning breakfast would be coffee and whatever was left in their saddlebags. Holmes was anxious to be on his way. According to the map Gilbert McCaine had prepared for him, a band of Ute Indians under the leadership of a chief called Walkara was camped only a few miles away.

The thought that his daughter, held captive all these months, might be that near, and that he was on the threshold of taking her back, had kept Holmes awake all night after their midnight crossing of the Laramie Plains. He had stood amongst the trees watching the sky brighten above the Laramie Range to the east, resisting the urge to push right on through to Walkara's camp and rescue the girl, knowing that Cross and Hampstead were exhausted, and that when the fight came, as he felt it surely must, he'd need his men well rested and alert.

He recalled his days as an officer in Old Hickory's army, and the long marches and pitched battles with the British in the swamps and backwater of Louisiana. He knew that men fought best when well fed and well rested. That alone is what held him here now, preparing coffee and a breakfast of the meager supplies they had on hand.

Hampstead and Cross rolled up their blankets, then came to the fire for the much-needed food. Afterwards, they checked their rifles and pistols, and reloaded the rifle they had found among the gear on Ozzie Warner's horse. Going into a hostile Indian camp, just the three of them, was a crazy enough notion. But if they must, Colonel Holmes was at least going to bring as much firepower as they could carry.

"Colonel, have you thought about what you're going to do if we *do* find this here Chief Walkara's camp?" Hampstead inquired as he sipped his coffee.

He had not. But he knew that whatever plan he came up with, these two loyal soldiers . . . friends . . . would follow him, even if it meant their very lives.

"Before I can know that, Chester, I must discover the location of the camp and reconnoiter it to determine the Utes' strength and weaknesses. If possible, I would prefer to use stealth rather than force. But whatever it takes, I will give, up to the fullest measure. I will have my daughter from them before this day is through!"

"Whatever you decide, Colonel, I just want to let you know that Caleb and me will stick with you."

All Kit could conclude was that, even though he and his partners had no choice but to flee headlong into the night, heedless of the dangers such a flight presented, the Cheyenne, on the other hand, recognized the insanity of giving pursuit under such perilous conditions. One misplaced hoof could bring instant death to rider and horse. They knew it, and they broke off their chase after five minutes, returning to camp. Kit and the others, however, waited until they had put at least two miles between themselves and the Cheyenne before pulling in their mounts and giving them a moment's rest.

"That was a close call," Gray Feather said.

"Too close for my liking!" Bull groused, narrowing a withering stare at their Indian companion. "And if we hadn't gone out of our way to rescue this Injun's mangy hide, we wouldn't of had it at all!"

Kit grinned. "This mangy Indian might just be of some good use to us after all, Bull."

"I'd like to know how."

"If the Utes have taken the girl, who better than to help get her back than one of their own?"

Gray Feather shook his head. "I already told you, Kit. My people didn't kidnap this girl. They don't go around stealing white women."

"What makes you so dadburn certain of that, Gray Feather?" Bull shot back.

The Indian frowned. "Well, if you must know the truth, Mr. Jackson, we Utes are of the opinion that your women . . ." he hesitated, then said carefully, "let me see, how do I put this delicately . . . ?"

The Colonel's Daughter

"Forget proprieties, Gray Feather. Out with it!" Bull growled.

"All right. The truth?"

"The truth."

"White women smell funny."

"What!"

"I said that white women smell funny. We Utes prefer the more earthy aroma of our own—"

"Kit! Did you hear him? Did you hear what that mangy redskin said?" Bull grabbed for the Indian, but Gray Feather clucked his horse out of the big man's reach just in time.

Kit rode between them. "Rein in that temper, Bull. Remember what it done to your friend?"

"It's all that toilet water and powder they put on," Gray Feather hastened to add, suddenly seeing himself on the precipice of yet another disaster. "It isn't a natural smell. That's all I meant to say!"

"A proper woman doesn't use toilet water," Bull shot back.

"They do back east," Gray Feather was quick to inform the big, angry man, in an effort to soothe his growing rage.

Kit said, "If you two sit there fighting long enough the Cheyenne are bound to come over that rise and catch you at it. Now come on, let's ride. I don't know about you two, but I could use a couple hours of rest, and I'm not about to get it until we're safely up into mountains." Kit turned toward the dark bulk of the Snowy Range, now not more than ten miles to the west, and kicked his horse into motion.

Traveling steadily west and south, according to the map McCaine had drawn for them, they covered miles of rough country that morning, pushing their way through stands of thick timber. Then around eleven they came upon a trail that appeared recently used by a number of horses. Holmes stopped to study the odd gouges among the foot- and hoofprints. Although none of the men was an authority on these Indians, they concluded that the marks must have come from a great number of travois, which was a common enough method of conveying large quantities of goods among the plains Indians.

Holmes frowned as he swung back onto his horse. If these were indeed the savages who held his daughter, their numbers were formidable. They followed the trace for most of the next two hours, expecting to come upon the Utes at every turn as the way snaked deeper into the mountains, and the land grew more rugged with every passing mile. Then all at once the trail swung around a promontory of granite and below them stretched a narrow valley of green grass, cut down the middle by a swift stream sparkling in the sunlight. The stream tumbled its way past thirty or so lodges of the Utes' camp circle.

Holmes drew to a halt. Then, retracing their steps, he took refuge out of sight in the trees that rimmed the little valley.

"There sure is a passel of 'em, Colonel," Caleb Cross noted with a distinct lack of enthusiasm.

"I expected as much," Holmes admitted. They tethered their horses in a thicket and quietly move toward the edge of the trees, drawing up behind a rock overlooking the camp. They hunkered down out of sight while Holmes methodically counted the skin lodges below, making a head count as best he could. One of the things that struck him right off was the vast herd of horses kept at the head of the valley, on the other side of a brush barrier. At least ten men remained near the corral at all times. Including them, Holmes estimated the Utes' strength at something around seventy-five men, and probably twice that if he considered women and children as well.

"I don't see Meg," Caleb noted quietly after giving the camp a thorough looking over.

The Colonel's Daughter

"I don't either," Holmes confirmed, his disappointment showing.

"Well, now what do we do?" Hampstead asked as the hopelessness of the overwhelming odds began to sink in.

Holmes's resolve never once wavered. "We have several hours of daylight left before night is upon us. We will lay low here and keep watch. Hopefully Marjory will appear and then we will know in which of those miserable hovels she is being held prisoner." He spoke with the sharp ring of authority that men would expect from their commanding officer. This was war again, and Holmes was prepared and anxious to enter the fray one more time, regardless of the odds against him. "If she doesn't appear, then we will have to take our best guess and go on down there tonight and find her."

Chapter Nine

The morning sun was already well over the peaks of the Laramie Range, beyond the plains they had just crossed, when Kit and the others entered the thick timber of the Snowy Range. They made camp in a clearing near a spring of clear water.

"We can use fresh meat," Bull said, taking up his rifle. "I'll see what I can scare up, Kit." He strode off into the surrounding timber while Kit gathered sticks for a fire and Gray Feather took the horses to water and began rubbing the animals down with handfuls of sage.

Bull wanted to be away from the others just then as he climbed a low ridge, thinking of his clash with Gray Feather earlier that morning. Sure, they had just escaped a Cheyenne war party by the skin of their teeth, and every one was strung up tighter than a catgut bow, but just the same, he had nearly lost his temper, and would have strangled the Indian if he had been able to get his fingers around his throat. Thankfully, Kit had been there to break them up.

The Colonel's Daughter

Bull found a seat on a ledge of rock overlooking a clearing below where the sun shone warm, and he made himself comfortable, resting his rifle across his legs. There were two kinds of hunters: the "stalking kind," that kept moving, hoping to flush game out of cover, and the "waiting kind." Bull was of the later persuasion, preferring to find a likely spot, such as near a game trail, and wait for food to come to him. He would have favored a smoke just then, but the smell of burning tobacco would make any nearby game wary of his presence.

Yes, it had nearly come to blows earlier, and it unsettled Bull to think how swiftly all his resolve had vanished. At that moment he had slipped back into the skin of that old Bull. That William Jackson of Virginia who had murdered a man with his bare hands. As he sat there, his thoughts revolved around to earlier days, and all at once the visions returned . . . and those voices, those unwanted voices speaking words out of the past in his brain . . .

"No!" he cried aloud, and abruptly stood. Below, a startled deer raised its head and stared curiously, then it turned back and bounced across the clearing towards the forest. Forgetting the visions, Bull threw his rifle to his shoulder and fired.

Kit glanced up from the flames he had kindled and grinned at Gray Feather. "Considering they're only eastern-bred saddle horses, you do an admirable job of caring for them."

Gray Feather affectionately scratched one of the animals under the jaw, then turned them out to graze the grass at the edge of the campsite. "They can't help it, Kit. They're just big, mostly dumb animals doing the best they know how."

"Mighty big-hearted of you to say so." Kit watched as Gray Feather turned to his heavy saddlebags. "What do you have in them things, anyway? Bricks?"

"Bricks?" He gave a chuckle. "You might call them that. Bricks to build the mind," Gray Feather said, as if testing out the phrase for future use. "They are books, Kit, and a few other belongings."

"Books? How many you got in there?"

"Oh, seven or eight."

"What are you planning to do with 'em all?"

Gray Feather removed a small bundle from one of the bags and shook it out. "I was hoping I might teach my people to read and write," he said, stripping off what was left of the clothing he'd been wearing when Kit and Bull had spotted him fleeing the Cheyenne. As he spoke he slipped into the leggings, and breechclout of a Ute warrior. He pulled on a beaded leather shirt and belted a butcher knife around his waist. "There, is that more appropriate?"

Kit frowned as he stirred the fire with a stick. "Well, at least now you look like an Injun. Still don't sound like one."

"Hail the camp!"

They glanced up. Kit said, "Enter at your own peril, Bull, and I hope you have food with you! There are a couple of men here who are hungry enough to eat saddle leather."

Bull came into camp with the gutted deer across his shoulders. The weight of the animal would have brought most men to their knees, but Bull strolled over and dumped it onto the ground near the fire as easily as if it was no heavier than a sack of potatoes.

"There you go, Kit. I shot it and cleaned it. One of you can butcher it." His view happened upon Gray Feather. "My God! We got us an Indian in camp, Kit!"

"It's nothing to fear, Bull. He's of a friendly sort," Kit quipped.

"All right, you two," Gray Feather said, bunching up his old clothes and shoving them into his saddlebags. "I've suffered enough grief for one day, and I don't need any more from either of you."

Bull laughed, set his rifle aside, and sat back against a tree, stretching out his long legs. "After last night, I'm ready to sleep for about three days."

"Well, you've only got part of one. I figured we'd rest up here today and get an early start in the morning," Kit said, cutting a thick slab of meat from the animal Bull had brought into camp. "We'll eat good today, boys."

Kit roasted as much venison as they could devour, and afterwards the men laid around camp, smoking and swapping tales. Later, Gray Feather took out a tablet of paper and a pencil and began scribbling in it. They were worn out from their all-night ordeal, and as the afternoon lengthened, they dozed on and off in the sun. Kit wished he still had his blanket, but it had served him well back at the watering hole, and he couldn't complain much about its loss.

After an evening meal of venison and some roots they had scrounged in the forest, Bull opened his thick volume of Shakespeare, flipped through a few pages, then looked across the camp at Gray Feather, who appeared to be dozing.

"Hey, chief!"

Gray Feather sat up. "Are you speaking to me?"

"Dang right I am, Mr. Harvard graduate in English drama. Let's see if you can cipher out this one." He looked into the book and read, " 'When sorrows come they come not single spies, but in battalions.' "

The Ute thought a moment, his brow rippling in concentration, then he said, "*Hamlet*, act four, scene five."

Bull stared at him in open amazement. "You got lucky that time." He turned over half a hundred pages, studied the book before him, then threw out another challenge. " 'Speak of me as I am. Nothing extenuate, nor set down aught in malice.' "

Gray Feather laughed. "That one is easy. *Othello*, act five, scene two."

Bull growled, grinding his teeth, then quickly flipped

over another hundred or two pages. " 'Men must endure their going hence even as their coming hither.' "

" 'Men must endure . . . men must endure . . . ' I got it, *King Lear*, act five, scene two."

Bull was on the verge of apoplexy. He grabbed a thick sheath of pages, flung them over, and spat out the words, " 'Of he who doth die the ignoble death, it is ye, the savage. Curses upon thee!' "

The cocky grin on Gray Feather's face remained a moment as if a frozen caricature in marble. Then slowly a scowl developed, and Kit could see the cogs in the Ute's brain grinding away. "Ignoble death . . . ?" he repeated three or four times, and then in defeat he shrugged his shoulders, looking embarrassed. "I am at a loss, Mr. Jackson. I don't recall that line."

"Ah ha!" Bull trumpeted. "Found one you didn't know!"

Gray Feather was genuinely disturbed. He sprang to his feet and started across the camp, but Bull slammed the covers of the book shut.

"Oh no you don't."

"At least tell me which play it was from. I don't understand it. I thought I had every major play memorized. It was an exercise that the Master required of all his students."

"Well, you must have missed one of them," Bull gloated, taking almost childish delight in having stymied the Indian.

Gray Feather stalked back to his blanket and sat down, staring moodily at the evening shadows inching across the Laramie Plains below.

"You ain't going to let him sulk like that, are you Bull?"

"Let him figure it out for himself." Bull put the book away, came over to the fire and got his pipe going. He blew a smoke ring at the tree branches overhead, then asked, "You ever remember something someone once said so clearly, Kit, that you can actually hear their voices?"

"You mean like something what happened to a fellow, say when he was a kid?"

"Yeah, I suppose that's it."

Kit pondered the question. "Don't know as I can say I actually hear the voices, but I do remember the words, and the way they was spoke. Like the time I first come west and a fellow in our party by the name of Andrew Broadus went and shot himself in his own arm. That wound festered up something fierce until it turned to gangrene, and we had to cut it off right there along the trail. All we had was an old saw and a razor, and a red-hot kingbolt to sear the flesh with and stop the bleeding. To this day I can hear him crying to high heaven when they started to cut on him, but I can't say that I actually hear his words sounding in my head. Not like some folks say they hear God a-talking to 'em. Why? What's chewing at you?"

"Nothing. I was just wondering, that's all. Say, what ever happened to him?"

"Broadus? Why, he was all healed up by time we reached Santa Fe. Didn't hardly miss the arm at all."

Bull went back to the pallet of pine needles he had built for himself and laid down.

Gray Feather was still sulking.

Kit stirred the fire, sending up a shower of sparks, then doused it with the leftovers in the coffeepot and curled up on his oilskin groundsheet and went to sleep. It was a restless sleep, and he dreamed of a girl with bright blue eyes and soft blond hair. The dream awoke him in the middle of the night and he lay shivering in the chill air, rehashing the night vision. The face had been the same face he'd seen a few nights earlier, just before he had drifted off to sleep. Kit wondered what it could mean. Was it because he was searching for the captive girl, Marjory Holmes, and his mind was merely supplying a face to put with the name . . . any face . . .

perhaps one out of his past? He thought of Bull's concern about voices speaking inside his head. Was this something along the same lines? And if it was, what strange forces at work in these mountains could have been responsible for it?

Never had the hours passed so slowly; not even on that long, sweltering day nineteen years ago when Holmes and his men had waited just outside New Orleans for word from the general that the time had come to move on the British. The hours that passed back then were nothing compared to those of this day as they hid in the rocks, spying out the Ute encampment below. Time dragged along as if tethered to a ship's anchor chain, and not once during all that span did they catch a glimpse of Marjory.

But it hadn't been a complete loss. Holmes had identified at least one lodge among the many down there that appeared to have a guard posted at its door. With the coming of night, the camp lit up with dozens of fires, but as the hours crawled by, one by one the fires went out until the camp slept peacefully in deep darkness, except for a small fire by the brush corral, and one among the lodges near the stream, where a couple of guards talked idly.

"Time," Holmes whispered, taking up his rifle and thrusting a pistol under his belt. Cross and Hampstead were both heavily armed. Hampstead carried not only his own weapons; including a butcher knife and a tomahawk, but Ozzie Warner's rifle too.

The men moved out of cover, circling wide so as to approach the camp as far from the two guards as possible. In a few moments they were creeping low across the open ground, then they were in among the deeper shadows of the lodges. They dared not speak now, so Holmes employed hand sign, to direct their movement.

Holmes crept toward the guarded lodge that they had spied from above, moving with light-footed care, as if the ground was covered in eggshells. Every few feet he would bring his small brigade to a halt and hunker down in the cover of the night, listening to the telling sounds of the sleeping Indian camp. This was far more nerve-wracking than anything he had ever done during the war. Far more deadly, he knew, for at least back in Louisiana the enemy was the British, a civilized people.

Hampstead eased up alongside him and pointed. A Ute warrior had emerged from the shadows across the camp and was strolling over to speak to the guard. The wait seemed like a hour, although only a few minutes passed as the newcomer took up his station and the original guard went off to his lodge.

"Changing of the guard," Holmes whispered into Hampstead's ear. This new arrival made a couple of turns around the lodge, then settled down to wait out his shift. Holmes heard the muffled voices of the two other night watchers by the fire near the stream, far enough away to be not a large concern. Easing out of their cramped position, they crept through the dark, drawing on all their skills at stealth. A few minutes later they stopped again, this time at the back of the lodge.

Holmes swallowed down a lump of apprehension. He had no hard evidence that his daughter was actually here, just on the other side of this dark wall. It was all circumstantial. But there was only one way that he would know for certain. He motioned to his two comrades. From their long years of friendship, each knew what the Colonel was asking; no words needed to be spoken. Hampstead and Cross each drew their thick-bladed butcher knives and took up flanking positions. If the guard chose to make another turn around the lodge, he would find the trip suddenly cut short.

Working with his own blade, the colonel began a slow and silent excavation of the ground. In a few minutes he had tunneled enough to push a hand beneath it and up inside. He glanced around. Still all was silent. His men were well positioned and alert. Holmes turned back to the task. Slowly the hole widened.

A frantic hand signal from Caleb Cross brought the work to a halt. The men froze as one of the guards who had been standing by the fire started across the dark camp toward them. He was carrying something, but Holmes was not paying attention to that. His view was riveted instead upon the large, dark dog that trotted at the man's heels.

Holmes slipped the pistol from under his belt as Hampstead and Cross readied their own firearms. The man and the guard began to speak in hushed voices, and with their quiet words came the odor of roasted venison which apparently the one had brought over to the other. And there was something else too. . . .

The low growl brought Holmes's neck hairs ramrod straight.

One of the Indians gave a short laugh and spoke to the dog, but the growl only deepened. The easy tone in the man's voice suddenly took on a more serious note. The dog started around the side of the lodge, his ears flattened, his tail low and stiff. At that moment Holmes knew they had been discovered. The hoped-for stealth of their campaign was lost and it was about to turn very noisy and very bloody.

Chapter Ten

From the warrior's throat there arose all at once the most hideous war cry he had ever heard—at least to Colonel Holmes's ears it sounded hideous. At that same instant the dog sprang, taking Hampstead by the jugular and wrenching the burly man as if he were a doll. So sudden was the attack that Hampstead never knew what had happened.

Caleb fired one of his pistols and the nearest guard reeled backwards, swallowed up by the shadows. The element of surprise had been lost and Holmes and Cross dashed for the perimeter of the camp. It sickened the Colonel to leave his longtime friend, but it was plain by the blood and the savage delight the dog was taking in rending his victim's throat, that Hampstead was beyond help.

Almost at once the avenues between the lodges were filled with men pouring out the darkened doors. Holmes darted aside, plunging off in one direction, and the last he saw of Caleb, the tall, wiry man was sprinting off the opposite way. Suddenly a knot of men blocked Holmes's escape. He swung the muzzle of his rifle around and its sudden boom and blinding flash was like a lightening bolt within the village. Holmes charged off in another direction, dodging and weaving, trying to make the stream and the open country beyond, but failing at every attempt. At each turn his way was blocked as he was being forced back into the Ute camp.

Some distance away Cross's rifle fired, then came the distinctive report of his pistol. Then all Holmes heard was the pounding of blood in his ears and the clamber of men swarming around him. He felt a tug at his sleeve and wheeled about, swinging his rifle like a mace. His attacker went down beneath the solid thunk, but in his place leaped a half dozen more.

Holmes blindly windmilled the rifle, momentarily keeping them at bay. Then something punched him in the thigh. It stung like a red-hot poker from a smithy's furnace. Holmes collapsed to his knees, pain exploding all along his leg.

Something struck him in the head, and the last he remembered he was being overwhelmed beneath a ponderous weight that crushed the breath from his lungs.

Holmes had no idea how long he had been unconscious. When distant sounds began to filter into his brain sometime later, he rolled his head upon his shoulders and winced at the sharp stab of pain that shot into his skull. He was sitting, he decided, and his hands somehow encumbered, but that was only a vague sensation, one swiftly overwhelmed by the searing ache coming from his right leg.

His eyelids parted to an indistinct world of gray light and air heavy with wood smoke. There was a dreamlike quality to the uncertain shapes of Indian lodges scattered about him, still half hidden in the gloom of a morning not yet upon them. Was it a dream, he wondered, trying to sort out the events which had led up to this moment. The smothering pain in his leg was real. And so was the broken shaft of an arrow, protruding unnaturally from a bloody stain upon the wool of his trousers. The memory of what had happened was a jumble of distorted images within his brain . . . until the vision of the dog tearing out Chester Hampstead's throat jolted Holmes to full consciousness. He glanced around again, spying the two bodies stretched out on the ground not far off, and the pack of dogs that sniffed at them.

A sickening despair spread over him as it all came back clearly now. The bodies of his two faithful friends were but a grim reminder of how he had failed them, and now he had failed Marjory as well.

Marjory!

Remembering his daughter and his mission brought his view instantly around to the lodge near the center of camp. At that moment the skin door was thrown back and a tall warrior stepped outside. He spoke briefly to the guard, then strode toward Holmes, bearing the mantle of authority as plainly as if he'd been a general crossing the parade grounds within his own fort. He came across the camp with the straight bearing of a proud and confident man, wearing much silver around his arms and neck.

Holmes tried to move, and only then discovered that his hands were tied behind his back, and that he was bound to a rough post driven into the ground.

The man stood over Holmes. Holmes reckoned him to be the leader, the chief of these people, and as such, he was the one Holmes would hold responsible for the kidnapping of his daughter.

In spite of his hopeless position, Holmes snapped out, "Where is my daughter?"

The vehemence of his attack took the chief by surprise. He stood a moment peering down at the bound and wounded white man, helpless as a baby, and an odd smirk came to his lips. When he spoke, it was in the Ute language, which as far a Holmes was concerned, might just as well have been Chinese.

Seeing that Holmes had understood not a word, the Indian switched to Spanish. Holmes recognized the language, but other than a few phrases, he understood none of it. The Indian frowned; then, as if his hand had been forced, he said in English, "Me Walkara, Chief. Why attack you my people?" His words came with much difficulty, and Holmes understood why the man had used it only as a last resort.

"I have come for my daughter."

Walkara frowned, not fully catching Holmes's meaning. "Daughter?"

"You, or one of your people have taken her captive, and I intend to have her back." It was bold talk for a man in his precarious position, but Holmes had already given up any hope of leaving there alive. The pain in his leg was murderous, and the pain in heart at the death of his friends nearly as bad.

Walkara shook his head and a necklace of silver conchos rattling upon his breast. "You speak of things me—" and here he inserted a word which Holmes could only assume was Ute, for he did not comprehend its meaning.

The chief turned back toward the lodge.

"Marjory! Marjory, can you hear me?" Holmes shouted at the open door. For his effort he got only odd looks from several nearby warriors who had assembled with their weapons. "Take your best shot, you red bastards!" Holmes shouted. "I have failed my family and my friends. I deserve nothing less than death."

The Indians spoke low among themselves, but made no move towards him. Holmes dropped his chin to his breast, and as he sat there gritting his teeth against the pain in his leg, a new sound reached his ear. It was a low, mournful keening of women, somewhere beyond his line of sight.

Holmes squeezed his eyes against the pain. Time became meaningless. All at once he was aware of someone near him. When he opened his eyes the sun had climbed above the rim of the valley and had eaten away the morning mist.

A woman was standing there, young, pretty in a primitive sort of way. Her eyes, however, were red and puffy, as if she had recently been crying. All at once she screamed at him, hurdling a vindictive volley of expletives that would have been recognizable in any language. Then she kicked his wounded leg. He let out a cry at the new rush of pain. She spit in his face, and would have kicked him again if another woman had not taken her gently by the shoulders and led her away.

Holmes rolled his head back, a wave of nausea washing over him, and he passed out.

Kit Carson surveyed the vast sweep of the mountains ahead of them from a ridge they had managed to climb, leading their horses most of the way, scrambling up narrow, rocky trails that often gave way beneath them, creating miniature avalanches at their horses' hooves.

"There's gotta be a trail somewhere," Kit said. "We just gotta find it."

"In any event," Gray Feather said, "this time of the year I think I know where we will find Chief Walkara's camp."

"Maybe the Indian's good for something after all," Bull carped, breathless from the hard push up the last several hundred feet of trail, fit only for mountain sheep and goats.

Gray Feather glared over his shoulder at the giant. "If I wasn't still searching my brain for the source of that quote, I might remember the way sooner."

"Hah! You're planning to run us up and down these here hills until we drop if I don't tell you, you scrawny excuse for a Ute! Well, forget it! Kit and me, we don't need your help. Do we, Kit?"

"If you two don't get off each other's throats, I'm liable to leave you both behind!" Kit said with feeling, but he was only talking. In listening to these two the last hour, he'd noted a change in their arguing. It had become more bantering than serious disapproval of each other, although Kit knew that Bull would never admit he was actually growing fond of the Ute.

Kit said to Gray Feather, "Where do you think Walkara is?"

"There's a valley about half a day's march to the south of here. If Chief Walkara is not down towards Mexico, he likes to make his spring camp there. It has good grass for all the people's horses, a natural corral for them up at the head of the valley, and plenty of game."

"You know the way?"

Gray Feather grinned. "I grew up in these mountains, Kit."

"So, why'd you ever leave them?" Bull asked with a tinge of sarcasm.

"My father came for me when I was twelve. He had moved back east, you see, but my mother had remained with her people. Father had helped outfit Mr. Lewis and Mr. Clark's expedition through a government contract. That's when he met my mother. But this life never really suited him. There was always the lure of money to be made. So, he went back to New York, made a fortune as a partner in a fleet of barges on the Erie Canal, then came back for me. I spent the next ten years of my life with private tutors, and finally had an opportunity to attend college."

Kit narrowed an eye at him. "So, when was the last time you were back here?"

"I've been back three times in the last ten years. It's not exactly a weekend trip, you understand. The last time was two years ago." He drew in a deep lungful of crisp mountain air, expanding his chest, then letting it all out at once. "And it is good to be back. The East is like a tight shoe, Kit. The West, well it fits me more like a pair of old moccasins, nicely broken in."

"You'd never know," Bull grumbled under his breath.

Kit stepped up into his saddle. "Well, since this here is practically your own backyard, Gray Feather, suppose you lead the way."

The Ute took the lead and as they started along a narrow game trail, Gray Feather said, "Mr. Jackson, maybe just a hint?"

"Forget it, Indian."

Kit only grinned as he fell in behind them, taking up rear guard.

The view from atop the Snowy Range was spectacular, but the trail that they had been following was better suited to mountain sheep than horses, Kit judged. Gray Feather had said there was a good, well-traveled trace farther on, but to get to it from the place they had entered these mountains, in their wild flight to escape the Cheyenne, required crossing some pretty rugged and dangerous countryside.

Kit had not seen any sign of man on this steep and narrow trail, but he had seen plenty of evidence of the abundant wildlife that lived in these mountains: deer, elk, sheep, bear, and mountain lion. Their signs were all over. As they rode, Kit's thoughts went back to a countryside so different from this one that it might as well have been on another planet.

It had been a few years earlier when he and a party of men had embarked on a trip to California. That other-world place had been the desert west of the San Francisco River and east of the Colorado. Now, with their horses tail to nose on this narrow trace with the bulk of the Snowy Range rising to their right and the depths of the Laramie Plains practically falling straight away only a few ticklish feet to their left, he recalled that previous trip. After four days of travel through that burning land without even the scent of water, the pack mules had strung themselves out in a line more than three miles long. It had been hard, miserable travel.

Luckily, they had found water on the fourth day.

Two days in camp to rest up, and then it was another four days without a trace of water until they reached the Colorado of the West, a little below that mysterious and unexplored Great Canon. So famished had they been on that trip that upon reaching the river, they purchased a mare heavy with foal from some Mojave Indians, immediately butchered the animal, and ate it entirely—foal and all.

Kit marveled at the variety of countryside that these vast western lands held, secreted away within the fold and stretch of mountains and deserts. There was even an ocean at the far end! He had heard tales of the wondrous lands to the northwest, hidden back along the Yellowstone River. A man named Colter had explored some of it once years before and had come back with such fantastic stories of what he had seen, it made Kit nearly itch with excitement to explore them himself.

As they rode the narrow trace, he listened to the conversation ahead of him. Bull was asking Gray Feather if he had ever read this book or that, and generally, Gray Feather had. Then they would spend a while talking about one or another of the characters, and the story line, or the author's style. Their talk made Kit's skin crawl. He preferred things he could touch and smell and see and taste. Not the obscure scratchings on a page, as impenetrable to Kit as if they had been the mystical Celtic symbols from the land of his grandfather, William Carson . . .

Suddenly Kit was aware of something he *did* understand. The hairs at the back of his neck began to tingle and his skin to squirm—and it had nothing to do with the conversation ahead. It happened to him sometimes when some danger was nearby. Kit never understood it, but nowadays he never ignored it.

His grip tightened upon the rifle across his saddle as his pale eyes stabbed into the crevices of the rocky ledge rising to his right. Then he saw it!

The Colonel's Daughter

"Bull!" Kit cried, but the warning came an instant too late. The mountain lion that had been crouching among the rocks along the trail leaped from a dozen feet overhead. Kit swung his rifle and fired, startling the horses. His bullet blazed a trail of fur into the air, but it had only skinned the big cat. The lion twisted once in the air, missed Bull as it came down, and imbedded its sharp, curved claws in the rump of his horse.

The startled animal reared, flailing the air with its front legs. On the narrow trail it danced dangerously close to the sheer drop-off to the left. Bull held on as best he could, fighting the reins, but the big cat's claws had sunk deep into the horse. Then the cat sprang away, tumbled a good fifty feet down the incline before it found footing on a whisker-thin ledge of rock, and disappeared.

It was about that same instant that the bucking horse flung Bull from the saddle and the big man followed the cat over the edge.

Chapter Eleven

Later, when thinking back on what happened next, Kit still had difficulty believing that a man could act so quickly, or so heedlessly of his own safety as Gray Feather had.

The moment Bull's horse tossed him over the edge, even as the huge man was tumbling through the air, Gray Feather sprang from his saddle, aiming for the falling man. They collided with the steep, crumbly slope at the same instant, but Gray Feather had been prepared for the impact. While it had stunned Bull, who had landed hard on his back, it only knocked the breath from the Indian.

But it did them little good, as they were both riding a slipping landslide of gravel toward the precipice and a sheer drop of hundreds of feet to a canyon below.

Clutching a fistful of Bull's buckskin shirt, Gray Feather stretched out his other arm and grasped the spindly trunk of a stunted pine tree whose roots had somehow managed to find purchase among the unstable slope. Bull started over the edge just then, and he would have plunged to his death, taking Gray Feather with him, had not the stunted tree, and Gray Feather's arms, held firm at the sudden jolting stop.

They hung there; the tree by the tenacity of its tough roots, Gray Feather to the tree by one hand, the fingers of his other hand locked into Bull's buckskin shirt with the huge man dangled on the edge of destruction.

Kit leaped from his plunging animal, the reins of the panic-stricken horse in a iron grasp as he stuck his head over the edge.

"Don't let go!" Kit called down.

Gray Feather cranked his head around until he could stare up at Kit past his taut right arm, through the sparse needles of the stunted tree. "He weighs a ton, Kit, and I'm just a scrawny Indian!"

Bull managed to look up. "You ain't no scrawny In-jun! Forget scrawny, for God's sakes. You're a heap big hulking, powerful Injun, and don't you forget it!" Bull practically pleaded, as the world seemed to drop away at the tips of his moccasins.

Kit instantly glanced around for some means to res-cue his friends. But there wasn't anything at hand.

"Kit," Gray Feather called up. "There's a reata on my horse."

Kit found the braided, leather rope rolled up tightly at the bottom of one of the book-filled saddlebags. He shook it out and tossed it to them. But it came up short. "Don't go nowhere," Kit said, reeling it back in. "I got a plan!"

"Better hurry," Gray Feather managed, his breathing coming in gasps as the strain was slowly working at his fingers. "Don't know . . . how much longer . . . I can hang on."

"Big strong Injun! Big Strong Injun! Just keep telling yourself that!" Bull had managed to get hold of Gray Feather's sleeve, but little good that would do if Gray Feather's other hand, or the stunted tree, gave way.

Kit stripped the reins from his horse and tied them around a tree at the edge of the trail, praying that the leather was still good. He tested them with his weight, and then slipped over the edge of the drop-off. The reins added eight feet to his reach. Looping an arm through them and freeing up both arms, Kit took aim with Gray Feather's reata and tossed it.

The coil of rope unfurled and its end came to rest a few feet from Bull.

"It's all I can give," Kit called down, stretching out at the very end of the reins. Bull released Gray Feather's sleeve and reached for it.

He missed.

Gray Feather groaned with the added strain. "Can't . . . hold . . . on . . . much longer."

Bull tried again, and this time his fingers found the rope. In a moment he had a hand around it and at once the strain on Gray Feather let up, transferred now to Kit, and the thin straps of leather that were all that separated the three of them from a certain plunge into eternity.

As the reins took the full brunt of their weight, Kit felt them stretching out. He also felt the sudden pull of Bull's weight in his shoulder and arms, as if he was being drawn and quartered. Bull began hauling himself up over the lip of destruction, and all that Kit could do was hold on, teeth gritted against the pressure. Bull came up the rope hand over hand, grabbed the reins, and climbed the rest of the way to the trail. In another minute, Gray Feather was making his way up the thin reata too.

Once back on solid ground, they collapsed, exhausted, rotating arms, necks, and massaging the brutalized muscles in their backs and shoulders.

Bull glanced at Gray Feather. "Thanks," was all he could say, although it appeared as if wanted to say more.

"Sure. It's what any 'heap big Injun' would do, after all. Isn't it?"

Bull half grinned, a bit of chagrin in it.

Kit stood and gave the big man a hand up. Bull rose stiffly, pressing a huge palm against his spine as he limped towards a wide spot ahead where their horses had found some grass to take their minds off the incident. Gray Feather inspected the wounds in the rump of Bull's horse and said that as soon as they reached his people, he'd tend to them.

Stiffly, they mounted their horses and continued on their way.

Holmes drifted in and out of consciousness all that morning. The wound in his leg had become a dull ache, and the skin around it felt as if it was on fire. The Utes had hauled Chester and Caleb's bodies away. Holmes had wished for at least a decent burial, but these savages most likely dumped them in a ditch for the coyotes to feed off. Well, what did it all matter really? Funeral ceremonies were for the living; the dead could care less, and in not many more days—perhaps today even—Colonel Willard Holmes knew he'd be with his two dear friends.

Dogs came by to give him a curious sniff and a warning growl. Young children, safely in the grasp of a mother or older sister, peered at him from round, dark eyes. Walkara came around about noon and studied him as he might an insect impaled on a needle. The wailing on the other side of camp grew louder as more and more women added their voices to the chorus. Holmes had already figured out the reason for the mournful sounds. Unlike his friends, the Utes were giving the men killed last night a proper send-off.

Little did it matter now, he thought. But if only he could catch one last glimpse of Marjory before these savages sent him on to the next world. . . . She must be bound inside one of the miserable hovels, he thought, or she would have come to him. Maybe she didn't even know he was here? The thought that she was being held by these savages was a keener pain than even the broken shaft of the Ute arrow protruding from his leg.

Later, a procession out of camp carrying the bodies of three men upon pallets took most of the people away for an hour. When they returned, there was a new electricity in the air and scowling men gathered in groups around him, cursing him, and spitting in his face. They hauled out the possessions he and his friends had carried with them and began passing them around. The rifles and pistols were prized over all else, presented to the mightiest warriors, he assumed. Walkara took a rifle and a brace of Henry pistols, and all four of their horses.

They ripped the framed portrait of Marjory from its leather case, looked it over, then tossed it aside as of little value to them.

"At least let me see my daughter," Holmes pleaded after they had ransacked all their belongings.

Walkara looked up. "Daughter? Daughter? What talk this?"

"You have her here, in your camp. You have taken her prisoner. I know I will die soon, but I beg you, let me say good-bye to her first."

Walkara cocked his head to one side, as if confused, then shrugged it off and carried his newfound wealth back to his lodge, commanding one of the warriors to lead the horses to the common corral.

The men stood around, grumbling, while their women kicked him and spat at him, and wailed unintelligibly in his face. This went on for an hour before once again Walkara emerged from his lodge and stood over him. He had put on a long, blue chief's coat with a white man's vest beneath it, and had added a bit more silver in the form of a belly chain, with no watch or fob. These, with the feathers, porcupine-quill bib, leggings, and breechclout, presented an almost comical picture. But Holmes was not laughing.

"White man come my village. Kill warriors. Why?"

Holmes was fed up with having to repeat himself to this Indian, but he did so again, hoping to make some headway with the chief. Afterwards Walkara eyed him narrowly then shook his head.

"No got daughter."

"You must have. You murdered the white trappers and stole the girl with them."

"My people no kill white man who trap beaver. No take white girl. Walkara smoke pipe with white trappers Beckwourth and leg-of-wood Smith. Ride California. Steal horses. Get drunk. Have good time. No kill!" He turned abruptly away and held court with his senior warriors, each as gaudily dressed as their chief. The talk went on for almost half an hour with lots of finger-pointing and war lances jabbing—all in Holmes's direction. The outlook was grim, but then Holmes had already given up any hope of leaving this place alive.

Then Walkara gave a command and a dozen men encircled Holmes. One of then drew a knife and cut the thong holding his hands to the post. Roughly, they jerked him to his feet and crowded around him, shoving him toward the edge of camp.

His leg exploded in pain and fresh blood moistened the crusted stain on his leg. Voices rose throughout the village as people from every corner joined in the mob. Dogs barked and romped ahead, sensing the excitement that churned in the crowd. Holmes staggered and fell. Unable to catch himself, he slammed into the ground, driving the arrow's shaft deeper into his leg.

They caught him up by his hands, which were still tied behind him, nearly wrenching his arms from his shoulder joints, then shoved him ahead. They finally pulled him to a stop near a tree, and slicing the bindings about his hands, they stripped off his shirt and tied new, longer straps to his wrists. A pair of men climbed the tree and several more below hoisted Holmes up and held him there as these new bindings were fastened in the branches above.

Pushing back now to make room, the mob opened up to view Holmes hanging there, his feet dangling a yard above the trampled grass. One of the young men swung up on a pony, rode out into the valley, and giving a fierce shout, lowered his war lance and kicked the animal into motion. Holmes watched the warrior bear down at him, the long, iron point of the lance aimed at his heart. As the rider pounded closer, Holmes shut his eyes to wait for the end.

Instead of impaling Holmes, though, the rider shifted the lance at the last instant as he rose past and delivered a solid smack with it across Holmes's chest.

The Indian gave forth a high-pitched yipping as he reined his horse to a halt and turned back. At that same time a second warrior rode out into the valley, turned, and lowering his war lance, repeated the false attack, again giving Holmes a brutal whack as he pounded past.

All the while, the people kept up a constant chattering almost as if cheering, although it was unlike anything Holmes could ever remember hearing in the world he was familiar with. The young riders continued coming. Six, seven, eight . . . Holmes lost track.

Suddenly the camp grew deathly silent. Holmes rolled his head forward and blinked to clear his clouded vision. The sun blazed overhead, stinging his eyes. Something had changed. The crowd was suddenly still as church mice, every eye upon a single rider, who had appeared from among the lodges from which Holmes had earlier heard the mournful wailing.

This rider halted in front of Holmes, glaring at him with pure hate in his eyes. Stretching the war lance out, he pierced Holmes's skin above the heart with its point and inscribed a bloody circle in his flesh. Holmes winced, but his body was already numbed, and the agony of this added infliction was lost among the all the other sufferings he had already endured.

The man kicked his horse into motion, and riding a few hundred feet out into the valley, turned and lowered the lance as the others had. Only this time the crowd was silent, and Holmes sensed that the rider would not pass him by with a mere slap. He blinked the sweat from his eyes, regretting that he had failed in his mission, and that he would never see his wife and children again. Regretting the deaths of his friends, but most of all, regretting that he had not rescued his daughter.

Then the rider drove his heels into the animal's flanks and the final charge began.

"How much farther?" Kit asked. They had ridden out the morning and were making good progress at chipping away the afternoon. The near plunge off the mountainside had sobered them up, and neither Bull nor Gray Feather had resumed their verbal sparring. Bull rode ahead of Kit, stiff in the saddle, as if every muscle in his body ached. And whenever he glanced back, there was that far-off look in his eyes, the look a man sometimes gets after glimpsing the grim reaper standing at his door.

"Not far," the Ute called back. "Less than a mile, if I judge it right."

"And if you judge it wrong?"

Gray Feather grinned back at him. "Could be five hundred miles if Chief Walkara has taken a fancy to move his people down into the southern Rockies." He reined up and pointed ahead. "That looks like smoke beyond those trees."

Kit leaned forward in his saddle, studying the sign. "It is indeed, and it's from a lot of fires, I'd judge."

"There, what do you say now?" Gray Feather said,

puffing up some. "Told you I would take you straight where you wanted to go."

"You sure did. Now let's see if there's a white gal down there."

"I already told you, Kit, Utes don't abduct white women."

"Yep, I know. They smell funny." Kit clucked his horse ahead, taking up the lead. Around a bend in the trail, the trees opened up, and in a pretty valley below was Chief Walkara's village, laid out along a sparkling spring. Kit reined up to look the place over. Immediately his attention was drawn to the large crowd of people around a lone tree just outside the village.

"Looks like everyone's gathered up for something important, like for a church meeting or some such," Kit observed.

"Church?" Gray Feather peered hard at the activity below then settled back in his saddle, his mouth suddenly drawn into a grim, hard line. "That's hardly a church service, Kit. It's a public execution."

"Hmm. Wonder who the guest of honor is?" Kit frowned. "Bull, let me borrow that spyglass of yours, will ya?"

Bull handed it up to him. Kit pulled it open to its full length and put the glass to his eye. It took him only a moment to find the center of attraction; a man, bare-chested, dangling from the limbs of a tree. As Kit watched, he saw another man on horseback ride up, put the point of a war lance against the prisoner's chest, then suddenly rein his horse around and ride away.

It was then that the battered man at the end of the leather thongs looked up, and Kit saw his face.

"That's a white men down there!"

"A white man?" Bull said, grabbing the spyglass and putting it to his eye to verify what Kit had said. "I'll be! It *is* a white man!" Bull glanced back in time to see Kit's horse leaving a rooster-plume of dust in its wake.

"What's he up to now?" Bull roared as Kit's horse

114

broke out into the open and streaked across the valley floor.

"Trying mighty hard to get himself killed," Gray Feather answered.

At that moment, the Indian with the war lance began his charge.

Chapter Twelve

"Christopher, a man who doesn't pause and study out a situation is a man likely to get himself buried by it," Kit's father, Lindsey Carson, was frequent to admonish the headstrong, impulsive lad back on their farm in Boon's Lick, Missouri. And Kit had tried mighty hard to take his father's words to heart, but something inside him resisted them like the devil resists goodness. Not that Kit was purposefully willful; it was simply that, as goodness took no part in the devil's nature, it was not in Kit's nature to spend much time pondering a situation—especially one where a man was about to be impaled at the end of a Ute war lance.

Lindsey's words of warning rang loud and clear in his brain . . . and Kit knew that once this was over with, he was going to have to tell Bull that he understood what he had meant, and yes, he *did* hear voices!

But as it had been back on his father's farm, Kit ignored the advice now as he raked his heels against his horse's flanks. Even though just an eastern-bred ani-

116

The Colonel's Daughter

mal, the horse had a huge heart and powerful strides, and in a matter of seconds he had closed what at first had appeared to be an impossible distance.

The Indian began his charge, still unaware of the closing mountain man, concentrating fully upon the dangling target with the bloody bulls-eye cut above his heart, two hundred feet away.

Kit measured the shrinking distance. As he drew near to the Indian on his charging horse, he readied himself; and then, with the inborn timing of an athlete, Kit launched himself at the rider.

The impact took the Ute completely by surprise, so focused had his attention been upon the helpless man hanging from the tree. Kit and the Indian hit the ground hard, both men momentarily stunned, but with a resiliency born of frontier living, they recovered almost at the same instant. The Ute shook off the shock of being cannonballed off his horse and yanked a knife from his belt. Kit was only a heartbeat behind him. He'd lost his rifle in the tumble, but he still had his knife, so the two of them faced each other on equal footing.

The Ute lunged and Kit handily sidestepped the point of the knife, parrying with a thrust of his own blade. They were suddenly encircled by the curious crowd, but no one made a move to intervene. Kit dodged another thrust, catching the Indian's arm in passing and giving it a wrenching twist up between the man's shoulder blades. Instantly the fist opened and the knife fell from it, and in that same instant, Kit raised his own knife for the killing blow.

Just then someone grabbed his arm. Someone else hauled the stricken Ute from his grasp. Kit wheeled, fire blazing in his normally cool blue eyes, only to discover that it was Bull who had stopped him. A tall man in a blue chief's coat had taken the young Ute under his strong grasp. Kit recognized chief Walkara at once.

There was a general melee of confusion until Gray Feather stepped up and he and the chief greeted each other like long lost friends, which, Kit supposed, was exactly what they were. Later, Kit learned that they had played together as children, Walkara being only a few years older than Gray Feather.

Gray Feather explained to the Chief the reason for Kit and Bull being there, and when he finished, Walkara turned to Kit.

"Carson! Good to see you again. What is all this nonsense about a missing daughter? That is all that man could talk about." Walkara had lapsed into Spanish, a language both he and Kit spoke fluently. "I figured he was about half loco."

Kit explained the whole story to Walkara, exactly as he had gotten it from Seth Wilson. When he had finished, Walkara snorted indignantly. "It's a lie! We have taken no white girl, have killed no white man—except that man's two friends. But only after they invaded my village and killed three of my warriors."

"I reckon there has been a horrible misunderstanding, Chief Walkara," Kit said, sensing the peril that the man still hanging from the tree was facing.

"Maybe so, but he has killed three men, and for this he must die too."

"Do you know who he is?"

"No. Does it matter?"

At his side, in a low voice so as not to interrupt the conversation that Kit was carrying on with Walkara, Gray Feather was rapidly explaining the custom of his tribe. As Gray Feather laid it out for him, Kit figured he was in a precarious situation as well, having broken up a public execution on a convicted villain, the sentence apparently to be carried out by a relative of one of the dead warriors.

Nearby, the warrior whose honor it had been to carry out the execution was fuming and shouting his indignation at Kit. Thankfully, Gray Feather was not translating those expletives for him, although Kit reckoned by the twinges that came to Gray Feather's face that the words were none too pleasant.

Kit put his best foot forward and said, "Chief Walkara, I know you to be about the fairest-minded Injun in these parts, and you have one of the finest herds of horses in the whole of the Rocky Mountains."

Walkara eyed him narrowly, his face not revealing what he might be thinking. Kit went on unfazed. "It seems to me I might have made a small civil blunder here, busting into your affairs and all like I done."

Walkara nodded his head, wordlessly accepting Kit's appraisal of the matter.

"You see, I didn't understand what was going on. I just saw that that thar white man was about to be run clear through by one of your warriors. Well, you would have done the same had you been in my moccasins."

Walkara only listened.

Kit said, "I got me some tobacco, Chief. How about we mosey on over to your house and talk this over."

"Good idea, Carson."

"Er, think we could cut that fellow down and bring him along too? I'd like to hear his story before that buck sends him on his way to the ghosts of his ancestors."

Walkara considered the request, then gave an order and the man was cut down. Holmes could hardly stand, and two warriors carried him along as Kit, Bull, Gray Feather, and Walkara crossed the camp to the chief's lodge.

They passed a pipe and all smoked from it, except Holmes, who was propped against a fancy pillow covered in polished and painted porcupine quills, similar to the bib Walkara was wearing beneath the vest. Holmes was still in a mild state of shock.

After the formalities were out of the way, Kit looked at the battered man. "You're in a tight fix here, mister. Mind if I ask what you were thinking, coming into Walkara's village and attacking his men?"

"I had no intentions of attacking anyone, Mr. Carson. My only concern was the safety of my daughter."

"This daughter, her name doesn't happen to be Marjory, does it?"

"It is, Mr. Carson. I am her father, Colonel Willard Holmes. And I know all about you and your attempts to rescue Marjory."

"How would you know that?"

"I got the news from Mr. Gilbert McCaine, whom I met along the way. He was the one who told me that Marjory was being held by these Utes. He also told me of your efforts to rescue her, but when we discovered Mr. Warner's horse running free with an arrow lodged in its saddle, well, we assumed that you and your friends had been murdered."

Gray Feather gave a running translation of this to Walkara. When a break came to the talk, Gray Feather said, "Sounds to me like this fellow, Wilson, has run you all on a wild-goose chase."

"It's beginning to look that way," Kit said thoughtfully.

"Our intentions were not to kill anyone, Mr. Carson," Holmes went on. "We had hoped we could steal Marjory away from here before anyone knew it. There were only three of us. My God, do you think we'd be crazy enough to attack an entire village?"

"Walkara thinks you might be a little bit loco," Kit informed him. He looked at the frowning chief. "Seems we got us a bit of a problem here, Chief. Mostly from what looks to me was a big lie told to us right at the beginning." Kit had reverted to Spanish. "What do you figure it's gonna take to make it right with your people so as me and Holmes here can leave in peace?"

Aside, Kit heard Gray Feather whisper, "Walkara is quite fond of horses."

Kit grinned. "Would you and the offended families consider a string of horses as proper payment?"

Walkara's interest was suddenly awakened.

The Colonel's Daughter

Kit glanced at Holmes. "I suppose you could supply these people with, say, two dozen horses?"

"I could," Holmes answered. "Once I return home."

Kit looked back at Walkara. "Would that answer to the offense? Twenty-four horses?" and with a sideways glance at Gray Feather, Kit added, "twenty-four fine eastern-bred horses?"

A deal struck, Holmes was carted off and a Ute doctor cut the arrow from his leg. His bedside manner left much to be desired, but the poultice that was applied to the wound drew the infection away and numbed the area so thoroughly that after a few hours Holmes hardly noticed the pain at all.

As the wound was being tended, Kit and Gray Feather visited the families of the warriors who had died in the battle with Holmes and his friends. They brought a peace offering of tobacco, and explained the great mistake that had taken place, and the desperate actions of a father distraught over the kidnapping of his daughter. Then they presented the deal struck with Walkara. The warrior whom Kit had jumped was put off by being denied the opportunity to pluck Holmes's heart from his breast with the point of the war lance, but the promised horses went a long way with the families as far as atonement was concerned.

Kit and Bull were permitted to set up camp in the village, near the place where Holmes had been laid out on a sleeping pallet. Later, Gray Feather came by to see them. With him was an attractive woman with streaks of silver in her long, braided hair.

"My mother," Gray Feather introduced, saying her name in the Ute tongue, then translating, "Summer Lodge Woman."

"Pleased to meet you, ma'am," Kit said, doffing his battered black beaver hat. He judged the woman to be in her early fifties, and right pleasant to look at.

"Me too, ma'am," Bull added. "I owe your boy here

more than you can imagine. He's one brave buck."

Gray Feather said, "Enough to tell me which play that line was from?"

Bull scowled. "Don't push your luck, Injun."

Summer Lodge Woman held out the folded blankets she had brought along with her. Gray Feather said, "I told her how you two rescued me from the Cheyenne, sacrificing your blankets in the effort. These are gifts from her to you."

"Thank you, ma'am," Kit said, accepting them. "It gets mighty cold at night without a good blanket to curl up with."

She smiled graciously. "You are welcome." Then she looked to her son, who nodded his head in approval and spoke something in Ute. To Kit he said, "I intend to teach my people to speak English. My mother is my first pupil. Tomorrow I will meet with Chief Walkara to ask his permission to start a school in the village."

"You were serious when you said you came back to teach your people."

"Absolutely," Gray Feather said with rock-solid resolution, then he faltered. "That is, if Chief Walkara will permit it."

"He might not?" Bull asked.

"He would rather it were Spanish. He doesn't think there is much future in the English language. He is convinced that in the next few years the Mexicans will swarm up from Santa Fe, and that Spanish will be the language of the masses. As you have already seen, Walkara has taken only a passing interest in English himself."

That night Kit dreamt of a pretty, blue-eyed girl, her delicate face held within a golden frame of blond hair. She was wearing a blue and white checked dress that looked strangely like a dress Kit's sister Elizabeth owned, but the face was not Elizabeth's. It was the same visage that had haunted his dreams twice before since beginning this quest for Marjory Holmes.

The night vision jolted Kit from a sound sleep, and he lay beneath the stars among the shadowy shapes of the Ute lodges, wondering whatever it could mean.

The next day Holmes stood with the aid of a crude crutch and hobbled around a bit.

"I must be on my way as soon as possible," Holmes told Kit as he tested his stamina. He was doing quite well considering the abuse he had endured the last couple of days. Holmes was a man who had been toughened by the hardships of war, and still showed it. They were walking slowly across the village and suddenly Holmes stopped and stared hard at Kit. "Who am I trying to fool?" he said with sharp disgust. "Marjory is gone. I shall never get her back. It has cost the lives of my two dearest friends, and I shall never have them back again either. I've been on a fool's quest!" He spat the words out bitterly. "These people did me no harm, yet three of them have died. Chester and Caleb's only fault was their loyalty to me. How misplaced that turned out to be! They had family back in Missouri, and now it will be my sad duty to inform them of their deaths. It is time to end this fruitless crusade and accept the fact that she is gone, gone forever. It is time I get on with my life, however many more tormented years I may have left."

In the midst of deadly Indian skirmishes, or in the burning desert with their mules nearly dead and no trace of water anywhere, or even among the stories he had heard his father and older brothers tell of the brutal fighting during the War of 1812, Kit had never heard such bitter defeat in a man's voice before. He searched for some words to encourage Holmes, but nothing that came to mind seemed suitable. A few dozen feet away at Walkara's lodge, the skin door parted and Gray Feather stepped out, wearing a face longer than a mule skinner's whip. Kit could see there was something mighty wrong with the Injun. When Gray Feather saw them, he straightened his drooping shoulders and fixed a artificial grin upon his face.

"What's wrong with you?"

"Me? Whatever makes you think there might be something wrong, Kit?" he asked blithely.

"The last time I spied anything as long as that frown you was wearing when you come out of Walkara's lodge, I was a-looking at the Missouri River."

"That obvious?"

"Like knock-knees on a Scottish Highlander."

He gave a wry smile. "Chief Walkara rejected my request to open a school in the village. He said the notion was foolish; a waste of time. The people need to know how to hunt, plant, and steal horses. Learning English was low on his list."

"Well," Kit drawled, "it ain't like you didn't expect that answer from the chief, is it?"

"I had hoped he would be a little more open-minded."

"Open-mindedness, I have discovered, is in short supply among leaders of all people. Only one I ever know'd had a lick of sense about him was dear old George."

"King George the Third?"

"No, blame you. Get your head out of them English books. It's old George Washington I'm talking about!"

"Oh," he said, but his thoughts were miles away.

"There are always other places to teach, Gray Feather."

"Yes, I know. But it was *my* people I had hoped to help."

They started to walk again, and a gloomier bunch Kit could not remember ever meeting. Then Holmes suddenly pointed at what appeared to Kit to be a garbage heap.

"There!" he said with a sudden spark of life in his voice. "Marjory's portrait. I must have that at least."

Gray Feather retrieved it from the refuse pile and brought it to Holmes. "She was quite lovely," he said, handing it over.

The Colonel's Daughter

Moisture gathered in the old colonel's eyes as he peered at the painting. "Yes, she was." There was something depressingly final in the sound of that last word.

"Might I look?" Kit asked.

Holmes handed the small framed portrait to him.

Kit's jaw dropped. He had to stare at it again just to be sure. But there was no denying the truth. Marjory Holmes, the girl in the portrait, was the girl in his dreams!

And he knew something else too. He knew exactly where he had seen her before!

Chapter Thirteen

Seth Wilson had stared out the window long after Kit and Bull had ridden off, that morning now four days past.

"I think they're gone for good. They ain't coming back," he said finally, letting the oilcloth curtain fall back in place and turning away from the rough, glassless opening to face the two people inside the cabin with him.

"That was a close one," Sam said, taking up a cup of coffee that had been left on the table, half forgotten. It had gone cold. He made a face and tossed the gritty liquid into a corner of the single-room cabin. Sam's last name was Covin, not Wilson as Seth had told the trappers . . . but then that wasn't the only lie he had foisted off on them.

The third person there had slunk back into a corner, as if trying to put as much distance between the two men as physically possible within the confines—the prison—of these four walls.

"And you!" Seth Wilson roared, wheeling around and pointing a finger. "I've already give you warning what would happen if you spoke a single word out of turn."

"What was I going to say with him holding a pistol to my spine?"

Seth glanced at Sam, and the pistol thrust in his belt, then grinned. "You tried to run off, didn't you? I only keep you around anymore because you still pleasure me some. Hell, you'd think after all these months you'd come around to me on your own."

"I'll never come around to you!" What had been a meek boy's voice to Kit and the others who had just left was suddenly robust and feminine, and in it rang all the vile hatred that a woman could pack into such few words.

Wilson's short-fused temper suddenly exploded. He took two quick steps and backhanded her, knocking her into the wall. The girl's hand went to her cheek where a new red welt was rising up from a previous purple bruise. "I don't know why you got to be so pig-headed about this. You're my woman now, so you might just as well get used to that."

Marjory Holmes pushed away from the wall with cold defiance in her blue eyes. "You might have taken me away from my home, cut my hair, and made me wear boy's clothing, but you will never make me your woman." She spat the words at him as if they had been poison in her mouth. "You can overpower me and use me as your private strumpet, but I am not one, and never will be!"

"That's mighty bold talk for a gal in you situation," Wilson shot back. A cruel grin came to his face. He grabbed up a handful of her shirt and threw her to the crude rope bed. In a moment he had torn away the boy's clothing, and as Sam stood by grinning, Seth Wilson had his way with her. And when he had finished, Sam took over until both men were satisfied.

They left her there, curled tightly against the wall, sobbing, and they went outside.

"Don't know why I bother keeping her around," Seth groused as they walked to the stream to check on their traps. "She's almost more bother than she's worth. And now after those men come a-looking . . ." He shook his head. "I just don't know."

"*I* know," Sam said, grinning wickedly.

Seth had to laugh. "Reckon you're right. It sure beats having to wait until a man gets back to civilization, no matter how much of a fight she puts up."

"You know, Seth, this might not be a bad time to think about pulling up stakes. The stream is about trapped out, and now that folks are looking for that girl. . . . How do you suppose they ever got on to her clear out here?"

That had been a question that had bothered Wilson since the trappers showed up. "I don't know, but you may be right. When the others get back, we'll pack up and leave. We've got a fat cache of furs to bring to market, and there are hundreds of little valleys where we can start over again. This time I'll make certain we're well away from any traces men might be using."

That evening, their two other partners returned and, crowded into the small cabin, Seth told about their close encounter with Carson and the others.

"I don't know how they got onto us, but I had to kill one of 'em when he discovered what was under that shirt," Wilson laughed, hooking a thumb over his shoulder at Marjory. "I managed to put it off onto the Indians, but I wasn't sure that Carson was completely convinced. I reckoned for a moment there we was going to have to shoot it out with him and his partner, a giant of a man called Bull Jackson . . . and it would have taken more than a pistol ball to bring that one down," Seth added, as if it was the most expedient way to describe a man of Bull Jackson's proportions. "I figure it's time to pull out of here. The more distance I can put between me and this place, the better I'm going to feel."

Russell Blackwell, one of the trappers who had been away when Carson and the others came, said, "You say they even asked for her by name?"

"That they did, and it almost knocked me off my feet. I figured we was in for a fight for sure."

"This is not good," Andre Leroux, the forth trapper, said. "I agree with Seth. This is the time to leave. Before others come looking."

Blackwell was frowning. "How could they know, unless there are people from her home out searching? Hell, that was well over six months ago. You'd think our trail would be cold as a Dakota winter by now."

As they discussed the problem, Marjory studied them quietly from the corner of the room where she had distanced herself, her knees drawn up and wrapped about by her arms. Her eyes kept returning to the pistol in Sam Covin's belt. It was only that pistol pressed into her spine that had prevented her from crying out when the trappers had come. Now she knew that with the trappers had gone her only hope. Was there really any reason to fear death? Wouldn't dying be the only release left from this horrible bondage? Either death by a bullet, or death in the wilds of this country. . . .

At that moment, Marjory Holmes made up her mind. Once, when Wilson and the others had been too drunk to notice, she had slipped away and set out her mirror and comb in the hopes of alerting someone to her plight. But if they moved on from here, any possibility of rescue would vanish. Up until now she had survived on that single hope, but when hope is no longer reasonable . . .

There was only one avenue left for her, and that was to escape into this hostile wilderness, where she would either be killed by Wilson in the attempt, or if she was successful, die by the compassionless hand of nature. Either eventuality was preferable to remaining with these brutal men.

The next day the trappers packed their animals, and

putting Marjory on one of the horses and binding her hands to the saddle, they left the cabin. They rode down the middle of the stream for almost a mile to throw off anyone one who might try to follow them. When they finally moved onto dry land, Seth started south for an outpost at the Old Pueblo, which he knew was near the junction of the Arkansas River and Fountaine-que-bouille. From there they would head into Mexico and trap along the Salt River. That, he figured, would be far enough away from this mountain cabin to give them breathing room. He'd heard the beaver was plentiful along those southern rivers, and that the Mexican government was right hospitable, so long as you got the proper permits from the local alcalde.

Kit and Bull threw a saddle on their horses almost immediately upon realizing the truth. They were tightening down the cinches when Gray Feather came over leading a short, muscular Indian pony. "I'd like to come with you."

Kit peered across the curve of his saddle at Gray Feather and was startled by what he saw. He actually looked like an Indian, replete in leather leggings, breechclout, porcupine quill bib, buckskin shirt, and a feather stuck into his hair. His horse was likewise outfitted in the traditional garb of a Ute warrior's animal, including the fancy silver conchos which, although not generally used by the Ute, were the trappings that Chief Walkara's mounted raiders preferred.

"Why? You're back with your people like you wanted."

Gray Feather tried to hide his look of disappointment behind an artificial grin. "Well, not exactly like I wanted, Kit. I had wanted to be a schoolmaster. But Chief Walkara dashed that dream."

"So you figure on riding with us instead?"

"If you don't mind. After all, if this Seth Wilson is

spreading lies about my people, I figure I've got a right to set him straight on the matter."

Bull glanced at Kit.

"I like his spunk. If that diminutive pony of his can keep up with our eastern-bred horses, it's all right by me."

Kit nodded. "You're welcome along."

Gray Feather swung up onto his horse. "Besides," he added, "I don't intend to let Bull out of my sight until he tells me which play that line came from."

"Sweet Mary in heaven," Bull groaned, rolling his eyes. "Maybe I spoke up for him too soon, Kit."

"I'm coming with you too."

They looked over to see Colonel Holmes limping toward them on his crutch, and leading the horse that Walkara had grudgingly returned to him, along with his rifle and pistols. The chief had retained all the other booty he'd taken from Cross and Hampstead.

"You think you're up to it, Colonel?" Kit asked with a note of skepticism.

"It's my daughter, Mr. Carson. You would have to tie me to my deathbed to prevent me from coming."

Kit admired the man's drive. Had Holmes's moccasins been on his feet, Kit knew he'd be just as determined to see justice done.

"We'll be doing some pretty hard riding," Kit advised the colonel.

"I've been riding hard all my life, Mr. Carson," he said, stifling a flinch of pain. "I'll keep up with you, but if I should fall behind, you needn't feel you have to slow up for me. I'll make out all right."

"I'm sure you will."

Walkara came over as Holmes was lifting himself gingerly onto his saddle. "The horses? When?"

"Just as soon as I have my daughter back, Chief Walkara. My word is my bond."

Gray Feather put that in Ute for the Chief, who nodded in acceptance.

Doug Hawkins

The four men turned their mounts from the village and rode off in a gallop. They had gotten a late start on the day, and it was many hours later, with evening coming on, that they spied the Laramie Plains far below them. Kit led the way, pushing on against the coming darkness. It was well into the night by the time the weary horses finally picked their way down a narrow trail that opened into the coal-black valley.

Throughout the day, Holmes had maintained their pace, gritting his teeth all the way. Kit had watched the man's strength slowly ebb away, but Holmes refused to stop for rest even at Kit's suggestion. Now, with a black stretch of thirty miles that lay ahead, Kit saw the opportunity to force rest upon the man in spite of himself.

"We won't cross this tonight," he announced. "We'll camp here and make an early start of it in the morning."

"Is that wise?" Holmes asked. "At least by night we'll have little to worry about from the Cheyenne. Mr. McCaine warned us of them, and your run-in only proves the danger is real."

"The danger is real," Kit admitted. "But then so is the danger of one of our horses putting a hoof in a prairie dog hole and busting its leg."

"I crossed at night," Holmes reminded Kit.

"Sometimes lady luck smiles, and sometimes she don't. If we did lose a horse, a man on foot, or two riding double, would be in more danger from a Cheyenne attack than four men on well-rested horses."

Holmes reluctantly agreed to the logic in that. They dismounted, made a cold camp, and after eating some of the pemmican that Gray Feather's mother had given them, curled up in their blankets and were asleep almost immediately.

The next morning, they awoke before dawn and delayed in the foothills just long enough to boil a pot of coffee. By the time the plains were beginning to gray beneath an only slightly brighter sky, the four riders were again on the move.

The Colonel's Daughter

No one spoke much, and every eye was on the alert for roving bands of plains Indians, scanning the horizon to the north, and the land ahead that stretched away to the ever-nearing Laramie Range. Kit remembered his last crossing, how the Cheyenne had appeared suddenly, and if they had not already been engaged in trying to run down Gray Feather, they would have surely spied Bull and himself, and the outcome might have been much different.

Morning became noon. A spring sun blazed overhead in a cloudless sky. Now and then the flat land gave way to sudden, steep washes which had to be carefully crossed. The plains were more broken up on this crossing than Kit remembered from their previous, more northerly passage.

Slowly, shadows lengthened in front of them. Kit kept an eye on Holmes, but although the leg appeared to hurt with every jarring step the horse took, the old colonel did not complain. A veteran of many difficult campaigns, for him this forced march was just one more to be endured. Kit admired the man, but then the colonel had his reasons. Both love and vengeance are fierce motivations.

The plains became more rolling as the riders neared the foothills of the Laramie Range. Soon, their horses dipped into a wide wash, where a trickle of water came down from the mountains on its way to the Laramie River, which they had crossed some hours back. They stopped to let the animals drink and to splash the dust from their faces and hands. Afterwards, with a growing reassurance that they had made the crossing safely, they pressed on for the mountains ahead.

Chapter Fourteen

A few scattered trees were all that marked their passage from the plains to the mountains. Ahead of them lay a desolate stretch of grass and shrubbery through which a fire had recently raged. Scattered across the ground were the charred remains of a recent forest, looking to Kit as if a giant had tossed out a handful of used matchsticks. Their mounts began picking their way around the fallen trees.

Bursting suddenly from the mouth of a ravine that had been all but invisible to the four riders, more than a dozen warriors swooped onto the burnt plains. Startled by the sound of their war whoops, Kit kicked his horse into motion, turning away from the oncoming war party and scrambling for a trail that snaked up the first ridge.

Kit suddenly realized the truth. The Cheyenne had been trailing them for several hours, pacing them some miles away, just out of sight, waiting for the flat land to give way to this broken country that would better hide their approach. And when it did, Yellow Wolf, still smarting from Kit's first escape and the loss of his warriors, made his move.

They had been caught off guard, and in a place where it was impossible to run free. An arrow zinged over Kit's horse, another thumped into a blackened tree trunk as he pounded past, urging his horse into a reckless gallop. The Cheyennes couldn't have picked a better place for an ambush, for the littered ground held back their horses, and other than a few scattered boulders and the woodpile of charred tree trunks, there was not a stitch of decent cover anywhere.

Kit spied a boulder nearly the size of a small cabin, with three or four charred trees fallen down around it. He drew a pistol and, wheeling his horse around, fired at the nearest Cheyenne, knocking the warrior off his horse. Then, signaling his partners, he made a scrambling dash for the rock.

The others had begun firing too, at the same time urging their reluctant mounts over fallen trees. A barrage of arrows rained down around them as they fought for that last fifty feet and the humble shelter. Kit heard an arrow thump with a different sound and when he cast a glance over his shoulder he saw the colonel slump in his saddle. At once Bull was at his side, catching Holmes a moment before he slipped from the saddle. The big man took the colonel under one arm as if he weighed no more than a bundle of reeds, and at the same time brutally sunk his heels into his horse's flanks.

Kit fired his second pistol, and at that moment Gray Feather, mounted on his little pony, came dashing through the melee, swinging his rifle like a war club, braining a Cheyenne who had the misfortune to get in his way. That little horse of his leaped and dodged and scrambled over the fallen trees as if he did such antics every day just for fun. Gray Feather reached the rock first, dove to the ground, and giving the pony a slap on the rump, sent him on his way as he ducked behind a blackened log and swiftly ran a ball down the barrel of his rifle.

Kit turned back toward Bull. His horse was being slowed by the Colonel's extra weight. More Cheyenne were spilling out of the ravine, and then Kit spotted Yellow Wolf. The war chief had halted just beyond the field of burnt trees, watching as his braves pressed the attack.

"Make it quick, Bull!" Kit shouted, putting his rifle to his shoulder.

"Damn horse!" Bull growled, finally giving up on the struggling animal. He swung off it, hitched Holmes into both arms, and made a rush on foot for the rock.

Kit picked up a Cheyenne dog soldier in his front sight and touched the trigger. A hundred feet away the rider flipped off his horse as if hit by a charging buffalo. A second Cheyenne materialized suddenly at Kit's left. He had but a heartbeat to flatten himself along his horse's neck before the arrow left the Cheyenne's bow and buzzed past his head. Both Kit's pistols and his rifle were empty and as the Cheyenne fitted another arrow to the string, a third dog soldier charged up.

Kit drew his tomahawk and, whirling his horse, hammered down with the short ax, cleaving the warrior's brisket. Yanking it free, Kit reined back to his first attacker. This time the Cheyenne didn't intend to miss. Kit's only weapon was his tomahawk, and as he hitched back his arm to fling it a rifle boomed and the Indian flipped backwards off the horse, releasing the arrow in a harmless arc across the sky.

Gray Feather gave Kit a quick wave then immediately poured another charge down the rifle barrel and chased it with a patched ball.

Kit dodged attacking Cheyenne, swinging his rifle like a shillelagh, until Bull had finally made it to the safety of the rock, then he reined his horse around to make a dash. From the barricade of fallen trees, two rifle shots cracked and a brace of dog soldiers that were about to overtake Kit went down on either side of him.

Kit leaped from his saddle and clambered up over charred logs and down into the makeshift fort with the solid granite boulder at their backs.

"Thought you'd finally bought the farm, Kit," Bull remarked, shouldering his rifle and picking up a dog soldier in his sights. The rifle boomed. Gray Feather's rifle hammered another Cheyenne off his horse. Kit reloaded his rifle, and shoved its barrel through a gap between two blackened tree trunks. He searched for his target, finally locating him still astride his pony, well out of range. Kit couldn't afford to waste powder and ball on such a long shot, and he shifted his sights and plucked another Cheyenne from his horse.

The Cheyenne kept up the attack until it became plain that they could not reach the trappers without meeting certain death. Yellow Wolf finally recalled his soldiers, and in that reprieve, Kit set down his rifle and turned to Colonel Holmes, who had propped himself against the boulder and had used his pistols to remarkably good effect during the attack.

Holmes winced as Kit took the pistols from him and eased him to the ground. The Cheyenne arrow the colonel had taken had entered his back, piercing the thick muscle, and emerging out the front.

"I seem to be making a habit of collecting these things," Holmes quipped, beginning to feel the full measure of pain now that the battle had temporarily subsided and defending their position was not foremost on his mind.

"It punched right through your bacon, Colonel. Looks like it might have missed your vitals."

"That's something at least," Holmes managed through clenched teeth. "I've seen gut-shot men die. God, I wouldn't want that to happen to me. I'd rather have it through the heart than spend days in agony."

Gray Feather crawled over. "It should be easy to remove."

137

Kit drew his butcher knife and sliced into the tough wood of the arrow just behind the iron point. After a few minutes he had cut a deep grove around the shaft and snapped the head off. Holmes groaned and bit into his lip as Kit carefully drew the shaft out from the back. "That's got it. Now to stop the bleeding."

Gray Feather took a cotton cloth and a small pouch from his hunting bag, and proceeded to apply a poultice to the wound.

"What is that stuff?" Holmes asked.

"Old family recipe." The Ute grinned at him. "You see, we've been dodging Cheyenne arrows a lot longer than you white folks."

Kit left the doctoring up to Gray Feather and took his rifle back to the barricade of burnt logs, crawling up alongside Bull. "Is the colonel going to make it, Kit?"

"He got lucky. That arrow only hit muscle." Kit glanced through the gap in the logs. "What's going on out there?"

"Nothing, since Yellow Wolf called his boys back. He must have figured it was costing too much to root us out of here."

Kit searched the open ground in front of their fort. "I reckon it could be worse, Bull. At least we can see anyone coming at us—except from the back." He spotted Colonel Holmes's rifle a few hundred feet off, where it had fallen when he'd been struck by the Cheyenne arrow. It would have been good to have that extra rifle. Kit studied the battlefield and saw no Indians anywhere.

"Keep me covered, Bull."

"Where do you think you're going?"

"To fetch back that rifle."

Bull frowned. "You watch yourself."

Kit gave his partner a grin. "That's what I expect you to do." He shoved his pistols under his belt, then handed Bull his rifle. "This has a mite more reach than my pistols, so you just keep them pegged back until I grab up the Colonel's rifle."

Gray Feather said, "It's a Cheyenne trick, Kit. They haven't left. They're out there, waiting."

"Well, wouldn't want to disappoint them none." He folded himself through the barrier, then hunkered down, making a quick sweep of the land. Still no Cheyenne. Kit moved out, crouching low and weaving from one tree trunk to the next. In places, last year's tall brown grass was nearly high enough for a man to crawl through unseen, but Kit didn't bother. If the Cheyenne were watching, they would already have spotted him.

He reached the rifle, grabbed it up, and started back. He'd gone only a step or two when the spine-chilling whizzing reached his ears. Instantly Kit threw himself to the ground, and a split second later, a Cheyenne arrow passed overhead. From the fort, Bull's rifle barked. Kit was up and running. A second shot rang out, then a third, and the next moment Kit dove through the chink in the logs and crawled to safety behind them.

"That was close," Bull growled.

Kit looked back at Holmes, who was leaning against the cool rock. "Can you still shoot?"

"Can shoot just fine, Mr. Carson. But it's the loading I'm rather slow at. I'll do better with the pistols than with my rifle."

Kit nodded.

"Mr. Carson."

Kit looked back.

"My daughter. We might be pinned down here for days. Someone needs to go for her."

"We aren't in much of a position to go anywhere, Colonel, pinned down here by more than a dozen Cheyenne. Besides," Kit added with a note of resignation, "our animals have scattered to the four winds. It would take days to walk back to Seth Wilson's cabin, and in your condition, it would take weeks, provided we could get away from here without the Cheyenne catching on to us."

Gray Feather was listening to them, an odd, far-off look in his dark eyes. It seemed to Kit that he was about to say something, then he changed his mind and looked back out through the barricade at the open ground.

"There's got to be a way," Holmes insisted.

Kit only grimaced as he moved back into position, watching for an attack which never came.

As night came on, they built a little fire out of the supply of twigs and grass readily at hand. The men were getting hungry, but they had no food. Both Bull and Gray Feather had had the foresight to grab their canteens before diving for cover, so water would not be a problem, at least for a couple of days. Holmes had fallen into a fitful sleep, and the last time Kit checked, the colonel was running a fever.

Quietly, Bull said, "I've been thinking, Kit. One of us should try to sneak out of here tonight and go after that girl."

"Been pondering the same thing, Bull." Kit looked over. "You want to go?"

Bull gave a short laugh. "Hell yes. If it would get me out of this pickle barrel we've gotten ourselves into, I'd go in a minute." Then he frowned. "But the fact of the matter is, you're the one who ought to go. You move faster and quieter than me and, although I'd never own up to it to another living man, you shoot better too, and that's all that matters now."

Kit knew that he could sneak away from there under the cover of darkness, but he hated leaving his partners in such a fix. Just the same, every time he recalled the terrified face of the "boy" . . . and every time he remembered that Seth Wilson had been responsible for Ozzie's death, Kit's blood boiled. He had to do everything in his power to keep his impulsive nature from taking control over him.

"You would stay here with the colonel?"

The Colonel's Daughter

"Someone has to," Bull said matter-of-factly.

Kit thought it over. "I don't know. If I go, that just weighs the odds more in favor of the Cheyenne."

Gray Feather had been listening to this. Now he spoke up. "If what you said about that girl being held by those men is true, then you need to go, Kit, and the sooner the better. After all, you did tell them you were looking for her, and you mentioned her name. They must know others will follow."

Kit considered, his brow wrinkling. "If it was me, I'd be pulling out of there just as soon as I could, and putting some serious miles behind me."

"There, see what I mean?"

Kit still wasn't convinced. But Bull put it to him another way. "Our water will last an extra day or two with only three of us drinking it."

Everything they said was true, but still Kit hated pulling out and leaving friends in a tough spot. "There's still the matter of a horse," Kit reminded them. "It'll take me days to make it back to Seth Wilson's cabin."

That odd look returned to Gray Feather's eyes. "What would you say if I could get you a horse?"

"I'd say you was a right clever fellow, and handy to have along, Mr. Gray Feather Smith. But I don't see how you're going to manage it without walking down to that Cheyenne camp and stealing one."

Gray Feather shook his head and grinned. "O thou of little faith . . ."

"Matthew, the fourteenth chapter, verse . . . er, verse something or other," Bull shot back.

Gray Feather smiled. "Very good."

Kit said, "Just where do you propose to get me a horse?"

"My horse, of course."

"Last I seen of your horse, he was making for the high country as fast as his legs could carry him."

"You forget, I was riding a pony trained by Chief Wal-

141

kara's Utes, and this side of the Nez Percé country, you won't find a better animal."

"I'm getting mighty tired of hearing how good Injun horses are," Bull grumbled.

"All right, say you can get your horse back. Why not ride out of here yourself? Our problems aren't yours."

"You risked your life to save mine, Kit. I figure I owe it to you and Bull to stick by you now."

"We only did it because we thought you were white," Bull growled, but Kit detected a note of regret in his words, even though the big man had tried hard to cover it with a rough tone.

"You want to know the truth, then?" Gray Feather asked. "The truth is, I'm staying right here until Bull tells me the name of the play he got that line from. It's plain as that."

Bull grinned. "I reckon then he's staying till the end, Kit."

Kit thought it over, then glanced out into the darkness where not even a flicker of a campfire gave away the Cheyenne position. He looked back at Holmes, turning restlessly upon the ground. It was true; If he left, their water would last longer, and holed up like they were, there was little the Cheyenne could do to get to them without eating lead for their efforts.

"All right. I'll go."

Gray Feather grinned and set his rifle aside. Kit killed the fire, and in the sudden blackness, the Ute slipped through the tumbled logs and disappeared into the night. Kit listened but heard no sounds—nothing, that is, except a snatch of a high whistle swiftly rising out of his range of hearing, followed by a hoot that might have passed as an owl to all but the keenest ear. A minute passed, then five. Kit glanced at Bull, who gave a frown and a shake of his great, shaggy head.

"The Injun was just talking through his hat," Bull said.

But then came the distant sound of hooves. It was the

cautious gait of an animal coming through the dark, and the next minute Gray Feather's face appeared through the chinks. "He's here," the Indian whispered.

"I don't believe it," Bull said.

Kit wormed his way out. Gray Feather was standing there, holding the reins of the little gray pony. Kit swung up onto the animal, his feet finding the flimsy leather stirrups of the light girdle that passed for a saddle. The horse high-stepped a moment, not certain that he wanted the white man upon his back, but a soft, reassuring sound from Gray Feather settled him down at once.

"I'll be back," Kit said, gathering up the reins, which were attached hackamore-style to the pony's muzzle.

"We'll be here," Bull said.

Kit turned the sturdy mount away and rode off into the night.

Chapter Fifteen

It was early morning when Kit reined the pony to a halt
and slipped lightly off its back. He eased up to the ridge
where he, Bull, and Ozzie had first peered down at the
rude cabin in the wilderness. Now Kit studied the setting below, still in the shadows that remained in the
bottom of the valley.

He had arrived too late. No smoke curled from the
wattle and daub chimney, and the lean-to barn was
empty. No horses grazed out on the valley floor, no light
showed in the windows where a slight breeze ruffled
the curtain. Well, he had half expected it, all the while
hoping that Seth and his brother had not been spooked,
and *had* stayed. Just the same, Kit circled around back
and approached the building with the stealth of a stalking cat. He listened at the corner of the cabin a moment;
then, drawing back the heavy hammer on his Henry
rifle, Kit crept up to the door and kicked it in. As it
slammed back on its leather hinges, he rushed in,
crouching low and swinging the long rifle from wall to
wall.

The Colonel's Daughter

The place was as empty as an old cracker barrel. Kit rose out of his crouch and looked around. There was a crude table made from a dozen saplings lashed together. A few sections of tree trunks shaped with the blade of an ax had been their chairs, and against one wall four fat branches had been driven into the ground and had once supported a latticework of rope, making it into a bed. Now all that remained of it were the marks left where the rope had been tied to the cross pieces.

Kit was about to step outside when a piece of paper in the corner, with a small rock on top of it, caught his eye. Kit hesitated, then picked it up. Just as he had feared, the page contained writing. He went outside and sat on the log where a week earlier he and Gilbert McCaine had plied Seth Wilson with a jug of Taos Lightning, trying to get information about Marjory Holmes. The man had been lying right from the start!

Kit studied the paper, but it may as well have been blank for all that he could cipher from it. The writing meant nothing to him, although he knew that to Bull or Gray Feather, it might very well have told where the trappers had gone. He did notice one thing. The arrangement of the letters at the bottom looked vaguely like the letters on the back of the hand mirror he had found. But the mirror was in his saddlebags, on his horse, and there was no telling where it was now. Without it to compare these letters to, Kit could not be sure.

Defeated by something so simple that most children could understand it, Kit shoved the paper into his pocket and began looking for something he *could* read. It didn't take long for him to find it. Tracks.

There were at least four men, Kit determined, assuming that one of the horses bore Marjory Holmes. Presumably, the other six horses had carried their supplies and packs of furs. He followed the tracks down to the stream and crossed over. The tracks never emerged on the other bank.

A slow grin inched across Kit's face. "So, you think

you can put me off with that old trick," he said to himself, and considered Wilson's choices. To the north and west was nothing but a vast, Indian-filled wilderness. No place to sell a winter's cache of beaver. To the east was Sublette's new trading post: not a safe place to go to now that men from that direction were looking for the girl. The south was the only way left. There were a half dozen places a party of men might exchange beaver for gold, powder, lead, tobacco, and a hundred other things they would need for wilderness living.

Kit urged the pony on and within an hour he had picked up the trail where they had finally left the stream. There were eleven horses in all, and following that many animals was to Kit a little like an afternoon stroll along San Francisco Street in Santa Fe. He could hardly lose his way.

The trace continued south, angling always a little to the east until it finally emerged into the foothills of the Rocky Mountains, where tawny grass stretched away to the east as far as a man could see. From here, Seth Wilson's trail took a straight bearing, and there could be no doubt now where he was heading. Kit smiled tightly to himself as he picked up the pace. Wilson and his partners were still two or three days ahead of him, but the admirable little Indian pony drove on with seemingly endless energy.

He tried not to think about the friends he had left behind, but instead put his thoughts on what lay ahead and rode until the light failed him. Although he could have trailed them in the moonlight, he stopped anyway, made camp, and went to sleep early. He was up before dawn the next morning, and at first light resumed the chase, riding hard all that next day.

The thick pine forest they had entered hours earlier ended abruptly on a high-plains prairie. This was Arapaho county, and Wilson and his party had been following an Arapaho trail most of the day, ever since they had entered the vast forest which sat in the shadows of the towering Rocky Mountains and had no name—yet.

Wilson drew up to survey the countryside before him. Far to the south the Greenhorn Mountains stood low and dark upon the horizon. To the east a sea of grass stretched unbroken, clear to the Missouri river. There were only a few pioneer trails breaking that yellow-brown sea where herds of buffalo moved slowly across the land. The Santa Fe Trail, ninety miles south, was one of them, and it was where Wilson would head once he had sold their beaver pelts. Seth glanced westward, toward the towering snowcapped peak that Zebulon Pike had named after himself. The Fountaine-que-bouille was a little stream that issued from that mountain. It lay ten or fifteen miles south of this point, and Wilson was determined to make it before sundown. From there it was only a day an a half ride to the Arkansas River and the Old Pueblo. Seth got the party moving.

Sam rode up alongside. "Arapaho country."

"I know that. Make sure you and the boys keep your eyes peeled wide. Don't want to be caught with our drawers down. We'll camp along Fountain Crik tonight, where there's at least trees for cover. Ain't nothing between this stand of pine and the crik but open ground, so we have as much chance spotting a war party as they have of sighting us."

Marjory Holmes's horse was being led by Rus Blackwell, and as they rode out into the open, she found herself almost wishing the Arapaho would attack. And when she wasn't wishing ruin and damnation down upon her captors, her eyes would come back to the pistol tucked in Blackwell's belt, and a plan began to take shape. They would have to untie her at the end of the day's ride; they always did. They had never been overly cautious about keeping her from their firearms, for she had never in the past showed an interest in them.

But tonight . . . yes, tonight would be different. She

would likely perish in the attempt, but that, at least, was better than continuing on with these brutal men with no hope of rescue. She thought of her family back in Missouri, and her eyes filled as she knew she'd never see them again in this world. But her mind was made up, and one thing Marjory was not was a quitter, once a course of action had been settled upon.

"What's that?" Bull was instantly alert as he sat up, listening.

They had spent the first two days beating back minor skirmishes, each time killing a few Cheyenne until Bull and Gray Feather had begun to wonder just how many more could be left. Then a full day passed with no action, but each time either of them had tried to leave the safety of the little refuge, an arrow would be waiting to drive them back inside. Their water was almost gone, and the situation had gone from bad to intolerable.

Gray Feather had been assisting Colonel Holmes with the last of the water in the canteen when Bull sounded the alarm. Now he paused and strained against the background noise of chirping birds and chattering squirrels. "They're coming," he said, half whispering and glancing up at the wall of granite that stretched over their heads.

Bull listened to the faint sound of men creeping up the backside of the boulder, and his nostrils began to twitch. "You smell that?"

Gray Feather frowned. "They couldn't shoot us out of here, so it looks like they're going to burn us out!"

Just then a flaming torch dropped from above, clattering through the maze of branches and trunks. Bull reached out and plucked it from the tinder, crushing the flames beneath his foot. Immediately a second torch fell from above and lodged just out of reach. Bull was pushing his way toward it when an arrow thunked into the barricade and drove him back. Had not a branch intervened, it would have plucked out his left eye.

"They've found our Achilles' heel, damn them!"

"It had to come sooner or later, Bull. They couldn't go on much longer sacrificing warriors to our rifles."

"They could have starved us out!"

"That would have required more patience than Yellow Wolf has. No, the only practical avenue left to them was simply to burn us out."

Another torch found its way into the rubble heap, scattering sparks as it fell through it, and as the flames started to eat their way through the woodpile, smoke wafted into the cavity under the boulder, stinging their eyes and burning their lungs.

"Damn them . . . damn them . . . damn them! If they think they can just roast us like stuffed pigs, they got another think coming!" Bull thrust a rifle into Gray Feather's hand. "Keep me covered."

"What are you planning?"

"I'm gonna shag them sons of bitches offa that rock and kick their asses the hell outta here."

"Bull, you're talking crazy!"

But the big man didn't hear Gray Feather's words as he shoved aside a huge log and lunged into the open. Wheeling, Bull shoved his rifle against his shoulder and plucked a Cheyenne off the rock. As the man tumbled headlong at his feet, the giant drew both pistols and as fast as he could thumb the hammers, he knocked down two more men. Gripped now in a blind fury, he felt rage sweep in like an opened floodgate, washing away all concern for his own safety. He began swinging the empty rifle left and right, mowing down the onrushing Cheyenne until the rifle snapped at the wrist and the butt went flying. He heaved the useless barrel back and hurled it like a javelin, impaling a warrior about to loose an arrow at him.

Then a hornet stung him in the back, high up on his shoulder, and almost knocked him over. He staggered, then caught himself as two more warriors leaped out from cover. Bull ignored the pain, reaching down to grasp a blackened tree trunk as big around as a man's waist. Giving a grunt, he heaved it up out of the grass. An arrow thumped into the wood, then another. A third slipped underneath it and punched Bull in the stomach. Bull groaned and swung the tree like a gigantic fly-swatter, and roaring like a furious grizzly, he charged toward the startled war party, scattering them.

All at once his breath was knocked out of him. The tree slipped from his huge arms and he crumpled to his knees. Bull tried to stand up, but there was no strength left in him.

From somewhere a rifle shot cracked, then a sharp report as two pistols fired close together. The world around him went fuzzy, the ringing in his ears swelled to a roar, his vision blurred . . . and winked out.

As Gray Feather had helped Colonel Holmes from the blazing tinder pile and set him with his back against the rock, thrusting a pair of pistols into the man's hands, he could hardly believe his eyes. The giant was plowing through the warriors like a mad bull. His body took an arrow, and then another, but the man seemed unstoppable until the whistling shaft imbedded itself in Bull's spine, and the big man toppled.

Gray Feather shoved his rifle against his shoulder and fired, punching one of the Cheyenne off his feet. Holmes's pistols barked twice and two more Cheyenne went to join the ghosts of their ancestors. But it was too late to save Bull. From out of hiding a half dozen warriors sprang for the fallen giant.

Suddenly Yellow Wolf appeared in the middle of the fray. "Enough!" he ordered.

Reluctantly, his dog soldiers backed away from the fallen man. Yellow Wolf stared at Gray Feather, then urged his horse forward. They were at once surrounded, and with their weapons empty, Gray Feather knew he and the Colonel had come to the end of the fight. Yellow Wolf reined in and considered the young

The Colonel's Daughter

Indian. "Your people and my people, we are not at war now," he said.

"No, not this year at least, Strong Cheyenne Soldier," Gray Feather replied, addressing the war chief in his best Cheyenne.

"When you were this high," Yellow Wolf held his palm just below his horse's withers, "you stole two horses from me."

Gray Feather managed a grin. "Boys will be boys."

Yellow Wolf smiled too and nodded his head as if recalling a prank or two he had played as a boy. Then he turned and pointed his war lance at the fallen man. "He fought a good fight. A brave man, that one."

"Yes."

"The skinny man. Where is he?"

"Mr. Carson? He had important work to do and had to leave."

Yellow Wolf wagged his head in disapproval. "I have horses back now." Gray Feather saw that the trappers' mounts were in Yellow Wolf's possession. "Big man fight well. Such bravery is good. You and this man, I will allow to live. The skinny man who left, he is not brave. I will one day meet him in battle, and that man I will not let live."

Gray Feather grimaced. Yellow Wolf was letting them off the hook, but he had set his sights on Kit instead. "I will tell Mr. Carson what you have said."

Two braves rode up and dropped the trappers' saddles in front of him. Apparently, the leather goods were not wanted. Only the horseflesh. As the Cheyenne gathered their dead, Gray Feather felt a sudden heaviness in his heart and knelt by Bull, looking into the big man's lifeless face.

"Sorry it had to end like this," he said softly.

There was a flutter in Bull's eyelids and slowly they parted. "We get them Injuns?" he breathed, hardly more than a whisper.

"We got them, Bull. You saved us from them."

The big man managed a faint smile. "Tell Kit .'. . tell him that my friend . . . the one back east . . ."

"Yes?" Gray Feather urged when Bull's words trailed off and his eyes closed.

Bull's eyes fluttered again. "Tell Kit that my friend, he's going to be just fine . . . now. Kit, he'll know what I mean." Bull's eyes closed, and those great lungs ceased drawing in breath.

"I'll tell him, Bull," Gray Feather said softly.

He started to stand when all at once Bull inhaled sharply, and his eyelids parted again. "Injun?"

"I'm still here."

"You . . . want to know . . . about the play?"

"Yes. I would like that."

Bull grinned. "I made it up. Ain't no such line ever written by ol' Will Shakespeare." He laughed, and the sound of it died in his throat as the spark of life faded from Bull's staring eyes.

Seth Wilson's band reached the Fountaine-que-bouille with a few hours of daylight left. He decided to water the horses, then push on until dusk.

Marjory slipped off the back of her horse and held up her bound hands to Blackwell. "Can you take these off for a while? I can hardly feel my fingers any longer. You made them too tight."

Blackwell called to Wilson, "You want I should free her hands while we rest up, Seth?"

Wilson considered, but he must have understood that there was no place for her to go. "Untie her."

He worked the knots loose and Marjory massaged her wrists as she walked towards the cottonwoods that lined the creek.

"Where do you think you're going?"

She looked back at Seth Wilson. How she hated the man, hated everything about him. Brutal and unfeeling, Wilson had already killed three men since Marjory had been with him—at least three that she knew about—

and she had no doubt that he would do the same to her once she was of no more use . . . or pleasure to him. She knew something else too. There was going to be no rescue from any quarter, and unless she wanted to go on living under Wilson's heavy thumb, a slave to his lustful desires, now was the time to do something about it.

Escape or die, it didn't much matter to Marjory Holmes anymore. Her one consuming thought was to be free of Seth Wilson, and either path would bring her to that end.

Marjory came to him and her eyes flicked briefly to the pistol in his belt, then lifted to his ruddy, bearded face. "I got necessary business to see to, Seth," she said, putting honey in her voice, though she felt poison. "But maybe afterwards, if we got time, we might take a little walk back yonder." She left the thought hang there unfinished; a veiled promise, perhaps? Well, at least she hoped that was how he would take it.

Seth caught her drift all right. "It's about time you come around to me on your own. Go off and do you business. I'll be along directly."

Marjory stepped onto a deer path that led back into the dense growth of cottonwood trees along the creek. After a few dozen feet she drew up, her breath coming suddenly in short, panicky gasps. What had she let herself in for? She had stepped through a door, she knew, and there would be no stepping back. Live or die, the outcome would soon be upon her. Marjory struggled to control her breathing, fighting down a sudden dread that nearly made her legs turn to jelly. She put her back against a tree for support, for the security that somehow the sturdy feel of it imparted to her. But it was a poor second to the feel of a loaded pistol in her hands, she thought wryly.

Then she heard his footsteps, heavy upon the leaf litter of the forest floor. Frantically her brain searched for something she might use against this brutish man; some knowledge perhaps, imparted to her by her father. He had, after all, been a soldier. He, if anyone, would have known how to handle a man like Seth Wilson. But search as she may, she drew a blank. Her father had never spoken of war to her, and fighting was a thing he had instructed his sons in, not something for a girl to learn.

"Where are you?" Wilson said, impatience clearly evident in his demanding tone.

She tried to stop trembling, but couldn't. With nothing but her own feminine wiles to draw upon, she steeled against what might come next and stepped out onto the path. "I've been waiting for you," she said, watching him approach. To her great relief, he still carried the pistol in his belt.

"You finished up with your business?"

"All done," she said lightly, as if she had not a care in the world.

"Good, then we can get on with my business."

"And what might that be?" She hoped to sound playful, but instead the wavering nervousness revealed her true feelings.

Apparently Wilson didn't notice. "My business is to show you a good time, like I done before."

The repulsive thought nearly made her vomit. But she was strong, and she knew what had to be done. "Well, I'm right here," she said.

He engulfed her in his arms and immediately his hands went to her breasts. She cringed, but let him have his way with her a moment or two, hoping the excitement would numb his brain, even if it didn't have that same affect on other parts of his vile body.

Marjory forced her arms around his big chest, and she worked her hands down to his waist, then with a quick move she grabbed his crotch.

"Whooa," he said, delighted.

The next instant Marjory had a hand on the pistol in his belt.

Marjory understood pistols, how they worked, how

they should be loaded, how they should be cleaned afterwards. But just the same, her experience with them was quite limited, her skill on the level of a rank beginner. One thing she did know was that before one could be fired, it had to be cocked!

She'd only have an instant, and only one chance. Giving it a tug, she pulled the pistol free almost before Seth knew what was happening. And as she did, Marjory jerked a knee up just as hard as she could. Wilson groaned, buckling, and involuntarily releasing his grip. Marjory broke free and tried to cock the piece, but the hammer was too heavy. Her panic rising, she grabbed the hammer in her fist and hauled it back until she heard a click.

Wilson went to his knees, still groaning, yet in his agony his head craned up at her and murder burned in his eyes.

Marjory pointed the pistol, and in that instant all the pain he had caused her boiled to the surface. She pulled the trigger.

Nothing happened . . . absolutely nothing! The trigger never budged!

In his suffering, Wilson still managed to laugh. "Stupid fool," he said, gasping and slowly standing. "You don't even know how to cock the damn thing."

One click? One click? . . . there should have been two clicks! Marjory suddenly realized her error, and grabbed the hammer again, hauling it all the way back this time until it clicked into place. By then Seth was on his feet. He lunged at Marjory and she yanked back on the trigger . . . all at the same time.

The pistol roared and leaped in her hands. Wilson flinched, his fist grasping his side. When he looked at his palm, there was blood there, but the bullet had only nicked him.

"Can't shoot worth a damn, either," he growled.

Marjory flung the pistol at him. Seth ducked and reached for her, but she turned out of his grasp and fled along the narrow trail. When she looked back, Wilson was still standing there, glaring, but Covin, Leroux, and Blackwell had showed up to see what had happened. Seth pointed, and that was all she needed to see.

The trees flew past in her terror-stricken flight. A shot rang out behind her and the bullet tore a furrow in the shaggy bark of a cottonwood tree a few paces ahead. They meant to kill her, that was clear enough. She half welcomed it, but a part of her brain screamed no, and spurred her on.

They were gaining on her. Another gunshot echoed in the forest and she flinched, weaving along the trail until it suddenly came to an end. Looking around, Marjory had no choice but to plunge headlong into the woods.

Branches reached out and slapped her cheeks and snagged her legs. Her lungs burned, her eyes blurred from the sweat and tears that filled them. She stumbled. They were gaining on her now. Sheer survival instincts took over, but she was tiring, and men like those behind her knew enough about tracking to find her no matter how hard and how far she ran.

Then she could go no further. Her weary legs buckled and instinctively she stuck out a hand for a low branch to keep from going all the way to the ground. They were so near her now that she could hear their hurried steps.

It had at least been worth the effort, she thought, hope dying within her. She prayed now that they would end it swiftly, not draw her suffering out.

Then a hand came down on her shoulder. Marjory tried to scream, but a second hand clamped tightly upon her mouth and dragged her back.

Chapter Sixteen

Kit Carson had about as much trouble following their trail as he would a herd a buffalo through a farmer's newly plowed field. He'd pushed the stout Indian pony hard in his pursuit, but the little horse had a heart the size of the Louisiana Purchase and he just never quit. Kit gained a day on them by the end of the first day, and by the second, he knew he was closing in. He followed their trail through the great pine forest, and emerging at the same spot they had, he halted to examine their tracks. Judging by the angle of the trampled grass, and by the warmth still remaining in the manure, he had finally caught up with them. It was only a matter now of not proceeding so swiftly that he might overtake them before he was ready.

This in mind, Kit rode to the top of a hillock and scanned the open prairie. He spied the riders with their string of pack horses not more than a mile ahead. A small grin creased his face as his grip firmed up around the long rifle across his saddle. He knew exactly where they were heading now. Kit and his friend Charlie Bent had surveyed this whole area when Bent was making plans to build his fort on the Arkansas River, east of the Old Pueblo. It was familiar countryside, and now he cut to the east, to a trail that he knew of. Not only did he have to remain hidden from Seth Wilson and his band, but Kit was forever on the lookout for Arapaho. In an hour he'd worked his way ahead of the company of men and horses, and settled in a copse of trees to wait. When Wilson stopped along the Fountaine-que-bouille to water their horses, Kit made his move.

It was as Kit stalked through the forest near the creek that he heard the first gunshot. Angling toward it, he caught a glimpse of someone fleeing blindly along the game trail, and then he recognized the boy, Billy Wilson. But Billy ran not as a boy runs, but with the distinctive feminine gait of a woman . . . Marjory Holmes! Kit's suspicions had been confirmed.

The forest echoed with gunfire. Kit kept the girl in view and saw that she was tiring fast, and that the men behind were gaining on her. Weaving through the trees like a wisp of smoke, Kit came up behind Marjory just as she nearly collapsed. She had caught herself in the last moment. And that's when Kit reached around and pulled her swiftly to cover.

He'd covered her mouth to keep her startled cry from sending a warning to the men now only a few dozen feet away and shoved Marjory to the ground behind a rotting log, covering her with his body. His buckskin clothes blended with the withered leaves that littered the forest floor and, as he had hoped, the three men charged right on past without ever seeing them.

"Don't cry out," Kit whispered in her ear.

Marjory managed to turn her head, her eyes showing both fear and surprise.

"Can I let go?"

Marjory nodded her head, and as Kit's hand let up she said, "You?"

The Colonel's Daughter

"Marjory Holmes, I presume?"

"You know?"

"It took a while to figure out. Sorry I didn't get here sooner. I sort of got delayed back there."

All at once she remembered her predicament. "They want to kill me! They'll kill you too if they catch us!"

"I figured that was their intention, ma'am," Kit said, moving into a low crouch to study the forest, his senses keen as a newly whetted knife edge.

"They murdered your friend—Seth and that carrot-top beanpole partner of his, Sam Covin."

"Covin?"

"Wilson only said he was his brother."

"Hmm. He must have reckoned I'd not be too suspicious if I thought you were all just one big happy family, is that it?" Kit listened to the footsteps ahead. The three men had stopped their chase, obviously realizing they had lost their quarry somewhere behind. "You lay low here and wait for me."

"Where are you going?" The sudden panic in her voice brought a flicker of a grin to Kit's face. "Don't worry, ma'am. I won't go off and leave you. They aren't going to let us just sashay out of here, and anyway, I got a score to settle with Seth and Sam."

She grabbed his sleeve, her blue eyes suddenly intense. "They've killed before," she warned him. "They'll kill you!"

"They'll try, and that's about as certain as tomorrow's sunrise," Kit answered, drawing his butcher knife from its sheath. Then he was gone.

Kit knew that when a man went hunting bear, it was serious business. But when he went hunting another man, it became downright deadly. And hunting three of them at once was about as close to suicide as Kit figured he ever wanted to get. It was time he whittled the odds down some. So he grabbed up a stick from the forest floor and flung it away.

The sound riveted the three men's attention, as Kit

had hoped. As they started, Kit pitched a stone that ricocheted loudly off a tree in a different direction. The men drew up, looking around. Kit stayed low, crossing his fingers. They took the bait, dividing their forces. Sam and a man Kit had never seen before went off after the stick while the third fellow stepped lightly toward the other sound.

Kit singled out the lone man, paralleling him until he had moved within five feet. Still unnoticed behind a tree, Kit tightened his fist around the big knife. The man passed by and Kit stepped out behind him, swinging down with the flat of the blade just as hard as he could. The man collapsed instantly. Kit could have killed him as easily as crushing a beetle under his heel, but instead he sliced a thong from the man's buckskin shirt and tied his hands behind his back. He'd hit him hard enough that he was not about to wake up for a good long while.

Kit had not seen Seth all this time, and that worried him a little as he drew back the hammer of his rifle and checked that it was capped. Then Sam called to his missing partner, "Blackwell? Blackwell, where are you?"

"Where could he have got to now?" the man with him asked in a French accent.

"I don't know." There was a note of puzzlement in Sam's voice. "He'll show up," he said, looking around. "It's that girl I'm wondering about. How could she have just disappeared?"

"*Oui*, but even so, where could she go to, heh? Is no where. She must come back or die."

Sam gave a short laugh. "Her end will be the same either way, now that she tried to kill Seth."

Tried to kill Seth? Kit's respect for the lady went up a few notches as he slipped quietly through the forest.

"You hear something?" Frenchy asked, "the rustle of leaves, maybe?"

"It's that girl!" Sam paused to listen, and as he did so,

Kit circled around and stepped out from behind a tree, leveling his rifle.

"The last time someone called me a girl I bloodied his nose," Kit said easily.

Both men wheeled about, then froze at the sight of Kit's rifle covering them.

"Who are you?" the Frenchman exclaimed.

"It's one of them trappers who showed up while you and Blackwell were away."

"Where's Seth?" Kit demanded.

Sam inclined his head to the north. "Back along the trail there. The girl put a bullet through his hide." As he spoke, his hand worked its way back toward the trigger of his rifle.

"Dead?"

"No, she only skinned him some."

"Too bad," Kit said evenly. "Reckon I'll just have to take her out for some target practice after I'm done with you boys."

Sam suddenly grabbed for the trigger. Kit's rifle boomed and Sam's arms flung wide, his rifle flying as the bullet punched a hole through his heart. Frenchy brought up his weapon, but Kit was already moving, swinging up his rifle and catching the tip of the other man's barrel an instant before it fired. The bullet whistled past Kit's ear as the mountain man sprang for the Frenchman, butcher knife already in his fist. The two clashed and tumbled to the ground.

Frenchy grappled for the big knife, and caught it, but Kit clipped him a stunning blow on the chin with his elbow. In that moment, Kit drew back for the kill.

Seth Wilson's voice barked out, "You kill Leroux, she's a dead woman!"

His words brought a chill to Kit's spine. He slowly looked over. Marjory was caught in Seth's strong grasp, with the muzzle of his pistol pressing against her head, terror frozen upon her face. Poised just above the Frenchman's navel, Kit's butcher knife never moved.

"You got only one shot, Wilson. Use it on her, and I gut Frenchy here, then come hunting you, and when I dog a trail, I don't ever quit it."

Kit's words worried Wilson. "Let Leroux up and we'll make a deal."

"I don't make deals with vermin, Wilson, and I reckon that's about all that you and your partners are."

"Them's mighty bold words considering I got the gun."

And that was just as Kit had intended them to be. A pistol fired at twenty yards was liable to miss as often as it would hit, especially in the hands of a nervous gent—one already bleeding some from a flesh wound to his side.

"In fact, I reckon I'd rank vermin a mite higher than I would a man who would steal a girl from under her own roof and carry her away from home against her will." Kit spat on the ground to display his disgust, and hopefully to stir the fire of Wilson's anger a bit more fiercely.

The pistol shook in Wilson's hand as his anger raged. The Frenchman's eyes were glued to the fat knife blade. "For God's sake, Seth, let her go!"

"He ain't got the guts to step out from behind her," Kit egged him on. "Cowards always find someone to hide behind, or to take the blame for 'em."

"You'll be sorry you said that, Carson! Sorry you ever laid eyes on Seth Wilson!" He shifted the muzzle of his pistol and pulled the trigger.

It's what Kit had been goading him toward all along, and when it finally came, Kit was ready. He threw himself backwards as the pistol barked, and at that same instant, Marjory Holmes brought the heel of her shoe down hard on Seth's instep. The man howled, violently flinging the girl aside.

Kit had already worked out the details. He had badgered Seth Wilson into trying for the long shot instead of the certain one. As he leaped away from the Frenchman, his eye was upon Sam's rifle among the leaves.

Too late, Seth realized Kit's plan. He wheeled around, plunging wildly through the trees toward the creek, where their horses were waiting.

Kit grabbed the rifle and dug his elbows into the ground. He picked up the fleeing man in his front sight. Steadying the unfamiliar rifle, he drew back the hammer, set the trigger, caught a breath, and touched the forward trigger. The rifle punched Kit's shoulder and past the cloud of smoke Kit saw Seth Wilson stumble, but he caught himself, and then he was lost in the wood that closed in behind him.

"Damn!" Kit cursed the rifle under his breath. "It shoots high and to the left." Kit had been aiming at Seth Wilson's spine. He stood, then remembered Frenchy. When he looked, the Frenchman was just laying there, not moving. A round hole in his neck seeped blood, and his head cocked over at an impossible angle.

Marjory came over, hugging herself to keep from trembling too badly. "Is . . . is he dead?"

"Reckon Seth didn't miss after all," Kit said, frowning. He looked at Marjory Holmes. Except for the blond hair cropped short like a boy, and the men's clothing, she was indeed the girl of his dreams.

He gave a wry grin at that thought. "You all right, Miss Holmes?"

"All right?" A violent shudder gripped her small frame. "No, I am not, Mr. Carson. I wonder if I shall ever be all right after what I have had to endure."

He turned her away from the body on the ground. "Well, I reckon it was not a pleasant ordeal, ma'am, but you come out of it alive, and that's more than these two can say. Time is the best remedy for you now, time and seeing your father again. Someday it'll only be a bad dream."

"Father is here?"

"I left him a few days' ride north of here," Kit said

briefly, not wanting to burden her with the serious situation he had left him in.

When they had returned to the horses, one was missing. There were some spots of blood on the ground, but not enough to convince Kit he had done any more than wing the man. Just the same, Seth Wilson wasn't going to be coming back to make any more trouble . . . at least not any time soon.

Blackwell had a horrendous headache when Kit put him atop one of the mounts and tied his hands to the saddle. Gathering up the pack horses with their valuable furs, Kit and Marjory Holmes started back.

The whole way back, Kit worried about what he would find. Coming down the ridge onto the field of burned timber, his worst fears seemed to have come true when he spied the boulder and the charred pile of ashes that had once been their line of defense against Yellow Wolf's dog soldiers.

Kit rode ahead, and at the sound of his approach, Gray Feather appeared around the back side of the boulder and waved to him. Kit swung down with sudden relief.

"The Cheyenne finally left?"

Gray Feather's wide smile faltered and he said, "Yes, they rode out of here two days ago. We've just been waiting for your return."

At that moment Colonel Holmes hobbled into view, looking drawn and weak, but still in one piece. "My daughter, Mr. Carson. Did you find her?"

"Father!" Marjory cried out before Kit could answer him. She rode to him and leaped off the horse. Holmes threw down the crutch to sweep the girl into his arms. Tears streaked both their cheeks and Kit couldn't help but feel a bit of moisture gathering in his eyes as well.

He quickly blinked it away and said, "Well, reckon you didn't need my help after all. Looks like you have everything under control here. Where's Bull?"

Gray Feather winced, and Kit read the news in the Indian's dark eyes. "Where is he?" Kit said with sudden urgency.

Gray Feather pointed. Bull's broken rifle had been driven into the earth as a marker, and his battered, black beaver hat sat atop it, trembling in the slight breeze from off the Laramie Plains below.

"He went down fighting, Kit. It took a dozen warriors to bring him to his knees."

"Only a dozen?" Kit managed a short laugh. "I'd have wagered a year's worth of beaver they couldn't have done it shy of two dozen men."

"Yellow Wolf thought he was a brave man . . . oh, by the way, he thinks you're a coward for leaving and he has put you on his blacklist." Gray Feather gave a small grin. "Before Bull died he told me to tell you that his friend back east is going to be all right now. He said you'd know what he meant."

Kit sniffed, then tugged his hat back onto his head. "Every man has ghost from the past that haunts him. For some, it's harder to bury than for others." Kit glanced at the grave. "Bull finally got shed of his."

"Mr. Carson, how can I ever thank you enough?" Colonel Holmes had hobbled up behind them. He grasped Kit's hand and pumped it hard, all the while keeping an arm around Marjory as if he intended never to let go of her again.

"Don't need to thank me, Colonel. Seeing Marjory safe and at your side is all the thanks I need." Kit glanced up at the prisoner still astride the horse. "You can take Mr. Blackwell there back to the States and put him on trial. Then I reckon a stout rope might be in order. I calculated those pelts will fetch about two thousand dollars. Take them back with you too. I reckon it's the least those men could pass on to pay back some of the hurt they caused you."

They saddled up their horses. Kit was reluctant to give Gray Feather back the pony, but he wasn't about to tell him so. He threw his saddle onto one of the mounts, and remembered the mirror.

"I once told Mr. McCaine that I intended to give this back to its rightful owner, Miss Holmes," he said, handing it up to her.

"Thank you, Mr. Carson. Thank you for everything."

"That goes for me too," the colonel added.

"Going back to Walkara's village?" Kit asked Gray Feather as they prepared to leave.

The Ute frowned. "My hope was to start a school, but since the chief thinks it's foolishness, I'm not certain what I'm going to do now."

Kit recalled the paper he had found back at Seth Wilson's cabin. He leaned forward in his saddle and considered carefully what he wanted to say next. "You've got a real itch to teach someone to read, don't you?"

"I do believe being an educator is my calling, Kit."

"Hmm. I've been thinking of brushing up on my reading some." It was about as close as Kit could bring himself to saying what was really on his mind.

"Well, now there is a coincidence, Kit. I've been thinking I'd like to learn to trap beaver . . . the way the white man does it, that is."

"Is that a fact?"

"If you wouldn't mind, I'd like to ride with you a while."

"I'd consider it a genuine pleasure, Gray Feather," Kit said, starting the company on the trail to Fort William, which after all, is how this adventure had started.

DON'T MISS DAVID THOMPSON'S OTHER TITLES IN THE

SERIES!

Mississippi Mayhem. Davy Crockett's wanderlust keeps life interesting...but this time it may be a little too interesting. For when the pioneer and his friend Flavius decide to canoe down the Mississippi, they don't count on running into hardcases out to grab everything they have, hostile Indians who want Davy's scalp, and an old Indian myth that turns out to be all too real as far as Davy is concerned.

___4278-9 $3.99 US/$4.99 CAN

Blood Hunt. With only his oldest friend and his trusty long rifle for company, Davy Crockett may have met his match when he gets caught between two warring tribes and a dangerous band of white men—all of them willing to kill for a group of stolen women. And it's up to Crockett to save the women, his friend, and his own hide.

___4229-0 $3.99 US/$4.99 CAN

Dorchester Publishing Co., Inc.
P.O. Box 6613
Edison, NJ 08818-6613

Please add $1.75 for shipping and handling for the first book and $.50 for each book thereafter. NY, NYC, and PA residents, please add appropriate sales tax. No cash, stamps, or C.O.D.s. All orders shipped within 6 weeks via postal service book rate. Canadian orders require $2.00 extra postage and must be paid in U.S. dollars through a U.S. banking facility.

Name_____
Address_____
City_____ State_____ Zip_____
I have enclosed $_____ in payment for the checked book(s).
Payment <u>must</u> accompany all orders. ❏ Please send a free catalog.

DOUBLE EDITION

The West is Taggart's land–his gun his only friend!
JAKE McMASTERS

Bloodbath. They are a ragtag bunch of misfits when Taggart finds them, a defeated band of Apaches–but he turns them into the fiercest fighters in the Southwest. And then, on a bloody raid into Mexico, some of his men rebel, and Taggart has to battle for his life while trying to reform his warriors into a wolf pack capable of slaughtering anyone who crosses their path.

And in the same action-packed volume...

Blood Treachery. From the Arizona Territory to the mountains of Mexico, Taggart and his wild Apaches ride roughshod over the land. Settlers, soldiers, and Indians alike have tried to kill White Apache, but it'll take cold cunning and ruthless deception. And when a rival chieftain sets out to betray Taggart's fierce band, they learn that the face of a friend can hide the heart of an enemy.

___4271-1 $4.99 US/$5.99 CAN

DOUBLE EDITION
They left him for dead, he'll see them in hell!
Jake McMasters

Hangman's Knot. Taggart is strung up and left out to die by a posse headed by the richest man in the territory. Choking and kicking, he is seconds away from death when he is cut down by a ragtag band of Apaches, not much better off than himself. Before long, the white desperado and the desperate Apaches have formed an unholy alliance that will turn the Arizona desert red with blood.

And in the same action-packed volume....

Warpath. Twelve S.O.B.s left him swinging from a rope, as good as dead. But it isn't Taggart's time to die. Together with his desperate renegade warriors he will hunt the yellowbellies down. One by one, he'll make them wish they'd never drawn a breath. One by one he'll leave their guts and bones scorching under the brutal desert sun.

_4185-5 $4.99 US/$5.99 CAN

Jake McMasters

**Follow the action-packed adventures of
Clay Taggart, as he fights for revenge against
settlers, soldiers, and savages.**

#7: Blood Bounty. The settlers believe Clay Taggart is a
ruthless desperado with neither conscience nor soul. But
Taggart is just an innocent man who has a price on his head.
With a motley band of Apaches, he roams the vast Southwest,
waiting for the day he can clear his name—or his luck runs
out and his scalp is traded for gold.
__3790-4 $3.99 US/$4.99 CAN

#8: The Trackers. In the blazing Arizona desert, a wanted
man can end up as food for the buzzards. But since Clay
Taggart doesn't live like a coward, he and his band of
renegade Indians spend many a day feeding ruthless
bushwhackers to the wolves. Then a bloodthirsty trio comes
after the White Apache and his gang. But try as they might
to run Taggart to the ground, he will never let anyone kill
him like a dog.
__3830-7 $3.99 US/$4.99 CAN

WILDERNESS DOUBLE EDITION

SAVE $$$!

Savage Rendezvous by David Thompson. In 1828, the Rocky Mountains are an immense, unsettled region through which few white men dare travel. Only courageous mountain men like Nathaniel King are willing to risk the unknown dangers for the freedom the wilderness offers. But while attending a rendezvous of trappers and fur traders, King's freedom is threatened when he is accused of murdering several men for their money. With the help of his friend Shakespeare McNair, Nate has to prove his innocence. For he has not cast off the fetters of society to spend the rest of his life behind bars.

And in the same action-packed volume...

Blood Fury by David Thompson. On a hunting trip, young Nathaniel King stumbles onto a disgraced Crow Indian. Attempting to regain his honor, Sitting Bear places himself and his family in great peril, for a war party of hostile Utes threatens to kill them all. When the savages wound Sitting Bear and kidnap his wife and daughter, Nathaniel has to rescue them or watch them perish. But despite his skill in tricking unfriendly Indians, King may have met an enemy he cannot outsmart.

_4208-8 $4.99 US/$5.99 CAN

Dorchester Publishing Co., Inc.
65 Commerce Road
Stamford, CT 06902

Please add $1.75 for shipping and handling for the first book and $.50 for each book thereafter. NY, NYC, PA and CT residents, please add appropriate sales tax. No cash, stamps, or C.O.D.s. All orders shipped within 6 weeks via postal service book rate. Canadian orders require $2.00 extra postage and must be paid in U.S. dollars through a U.S. banking facility.

Name _____

Address _____

City _____ State _____ Zip _____

I have enclosed $_____ in payment for the checked book(s).

Payment <u>must</u> accompany all orders.☐ Please send a free catalog.